Alabaster Snowball
and the Naughty List

THE KRAMPUS CHRONICLES

Alabaster Snowball and the Naughty List

Gavin Brock

Matador
Unit E2 Airfield Business Park,
Harrison Road, Market Harborough,
Leicestershire. LE16 7UL
Tel: 0116 2792299
Email: books@troubador.co.uk
Web: www.troubador.co.uk/matador
Twitter: @matadorbooks

ISBN 978 1805141 358

British Library Cataloguing in Publication Data.
A catalogue record for this book is available from the British Library.

Printed and bound in Great Britain by 4edge Limited
Typeset in 12pt Minion Pro by Troubador Publishing Ltd, Leicester, UK

Matador is an imprint of Troubador Publishing Ltd

Dedicated to all kids, from one to ninety-two

About the Author

Born and raised in the Rhondda Valleys, South Wales, Gavin Brock currently lives in London. As well as being a full-time primary school teacher, he also provides musical direction for a number of theatre schools in London and the north of England during weekends and holidays. As a composer and lyricist, his work has been performed at the Other Palace and Theatre Royal Stratford East. Having been a writer of stories and songs since he was a child, Gavin is delighted to fulfil his dream of one day seeing his work in print. 'Alabaster Snowball and the Naughty List' is his first book for children.

Part One

LAPLAND

One

THE LAST SUNSET

Alabaster Snowball braved the glacial winds and, with a hand-carved piece of wood tucked beneath his armpit, made his way to the peak of Mount Haltia. Even on clumsy snowshoes fashioned from disused tennis rackets, it was mere half an hour's walk from the Grotto. The peak was the perfect spot to try out his latest invention away from prying eyes.

Once there, he stopped to savour the panorama. For a moment the grandeur made him forget the wintry gale stinging his cheeks. Few natural wonders could provide such a feast for the senses as the one lying before him, and his heart surged with pride until it felt fit to burst.

Beyond the snow-covered crest in the distance, the skies were dotted with tiny pink clouds. The sun was sinking for the last time. Soon, as every year, it would disappear entirely and – save for a couple of hours' twilight each day – usher in several months of darkness.

In the valleys below, lights began to appear from the buildings, evidence – were it needed – of the human-folk that seemed to lay claim to every habitable nook and cranny.

Mercifully, they did not know about the Grotto.

Nor would they ever do, if Alabaster had anything to do with it.

From his belt, he unfastened a drawstring pocket made from deerskin, holding it close against the icy wind. With a large gloved hand, he took a generous pinch of the glimmering powder within and rubbed it along the length of the board. Satisfied that it had been covered sufficiently, he turned the wooden slab over once again and laid it flat on the snow.

This should work just as well as it did on the Big Chief's sleigh – and what a rush it would be if he was right! As long as he did not venture beyond the perimeter and run the risk of being seen, nothing could go wrong.

Taking care not to overbalance, Alabaster placed his large feet gingerly on the board's surface and seized the rope tethered to the front. With a gentle kick behind him, the board – and its excited passenger – drifted down the gentle slope.

He was snow-surfing, as he had done numerous times before – but this time with a difference. With a gentle shift of weight onto his back leg, the board rose off the carpet of snow and levitated several feet off the ground.

He had done it! His latest adjustment to the snurfer (as he called it) was a triumph.

Not that there was anything wrong with the original model, of course, which had started off as a pair of skis welded together, and after several prototypes had evolved into something resembling a child-sized surfboard. A winning invention, Alabaster had known in his gut, befitting of Santa's top toy design award that year... until chief judge Bushy Evergreen pointed out a fatal flaw at the Grand Unveiling.

'Who is it *for*?' he had asked when Alabaster presented it for the panel's consideration.

'What do you mean, who is it for?' Alabaster laughed. 'Children, of course!'

'Any children in particular?'

'Why, all the world's children, of course! Name me one child that wouldn't love a ride on a Snurfer!'

Bushy remained unenthused. 'All the world's children don't live in the snow, Alabaster,' he replied. 'I don't think the children of Honolulu will have much use for a snowboard. Do you?'

The realisation that Bushy Evergreen was correct had hit Alabaster in the chest like the antlers of an angry reindeer.

'It's good to have a hobby, and it's good to have ambition.' Here, he regarded Alabaster with a strained expression. 'But you're a factory elf. Stay in your own lane, there's a good chap. Next!'

The snurfer was a flop. All that work for nothing. All his dreams of fame and recognition scuppered in an instant.

Disheartened and despondent, Alabaster returned to his factory duties, wrapping and packaging mountains' worth of presents each day, daydreaming and talking to himself while the cogs of his mind spun like a pinwheel. Then, after several sleepless nights, he hit upon the solution: Santa's levitation powder! There was not a child in the world, wherever they lived, that could not make use of a *floating* snurfer.

And what a joy it was to coast above the snow's surface, controlling the rise and fall of the board with a simple shift of weight from one leg to another, or by pulling on the rope.

As he steered himself down the mountainside, Alabaster experimented with the shapes and patterns he could make in the snow by lowering himself towards the ground and lifting himself up again. Each slice sent cascades of powder into the air like a fine mist. A glorious wash of snowflakes brushed through his hair as he traversed the peaks and valleys of the sparkling dunes, making him feel refreshed and fantastically alive.

This was so much fun! There was no way Santa would fail to see its appeal.

Alabaster was so busy imagining the rapturous reception his new toy would receive – not to mention the new portrait of himself that was certain to be hung in Santa's office, alongside those great inventors Shinny Upatree and Wunorse Opensleigh – that he did not hear the thunderous rumbling from above. A slate of snow and ice had broken away from the peak above him and hurtled down the mountainside, gathering more and more snow as it rumbled towards him.

He only realised the danger when the first lump of ice smashed into his shoulder. It was too late. A thick, blinding cloud began to envelop him.

In horror, Alabaster leant back and yanked the rope back and forth with all of his might. But the onslaught of icy debris was too much. Before he knew it, the avalanche had consumed him, plunging him downwards at breakneck speed.

While his thick, clumsy hands wrestled to keep hold of the rope, his body careered off sharp rocks. He was pummelled and thrown about in all directions until he didn't know whether he was upright or upside-down.

He closed his eyes, certain he would be buried in ice.

As the icy mass neared the bottom of the slope, he was thrust to the surface where he caught some sharp snatches of breath.

The next thing he knew, he was sprawling over the edge of a cliff.

Two

OVER THE EDGE

Alabaster opened his eyes.

Through a haze of spots and spinning lines, low-hanging grey clouds came slowly into focus while the wailing of an alarm bell rang furiously inside his ears. Letting out a painful groan, he clambered to a sitting position. Every muscle in his body screamed. It could have been far worse, he supposed; he was lucky to be alive.

He looked around.

The deerskin pocket at his belt hung empty, its contents lost to the fury of the avalanche.

'Oh, no,' Alabaster muttered. 'No, no, no…'

9

To make matters worse, he had broken the cardinal rule of the elvish community: crossing the border. To his knowledge, no other elf had ever dared breach the perimeter before. Not that it was his fault. He couldn't be held responsible for being swept away by an avalanche. Could he?

Santa was not going to be happy, that was for certain.

A few metres away, the snowboard's splintered nose poked through the snow.

Almost forgetting his pain, Alabaster scurried as quickly as he could to pull it free. Mercifully, it remained intact.

He tossed it onto the snow and stepped aboard... but it was no use. The force of the avalanche had long since wiped away any trace of levitation powder.

How would he ever get back up the mountain?

There was only one thing for it; he would have to climb back to the Grotto on foot. Looming high above him, the peak of the mountain seemed to sneer down its nose at him for being so foolhardy.

He was about to begin his long climb in earnest, when a strange whimpering sound made him look over his shoulder.

No more than ten feet away, beside the gnarled carcass of a winter tree, a small black dot pulsed against the snow. Some kind of animal. A cub.

Leave it alone, he told himself. *You don't have time...*

But there it was again, a high-pitched mewling noise like the sound of a puppy calling for its mother.

Perhaps it was lost.

Worse, perhaps it was hurt.

What sort of elf would leave a poor, defenceless animal to perish in the freezing snow?

Ignoring the voice within that insisted this was A Very Bad Idea, Alabaster followed the sound and, with every effort he could muster, waded towards it.

Approaching the creature, it seemed to get bigger, until Alabaster could make out a large pair of black eyes blinking out of the trembling bundle of fur, no bigger than a football. Fine white powder matted the strands of its shaggy hair.

'Hello, little guy,' Alabaster said, reaching a tentative hand towards it. Its front limbs were a set of paws, while its rear legs resembled the tiniest reindeer hooves he had ever seen. When he picked it up for closer examination, its racing heartbeat was detectable even through the thickness of his gloves.

'Are you lost, hm? Where's your mother?'

The creature, of course, did not reply, but instead nuzzled its nose against the elf's chest, presumably taking comfort in the warmth of his body heat.

There was no way Alabaster could leave him there. Besides, Santa would know what to do.

And so it was that Alabaster Snowball gently placed

the creature in his knapsack and began his slow ascent up the mountain back to the Grotto.

Santa would surely allow him to keep it as a pet.

Wouldn't he?

Three

SANTA'S OFFICE

'Absolutely not!' Santa's low voice rumbled around the office like a roll of thunder. The old man's infamously jolly face now wore an unmistakable expression of alarm. He observed the animal, the edges of his nose wrinkling with revulsion. 'Where on earth did you find it?'

Alabaster and Santa sat at an enormous wooden table, upon which the little black creature tottered about clumsily on all fours, sniffing with curiosity at the stack of handwritten letters piled neatly in one corner. Bushy Evergreen remained standing.

Alabaster hesitated.

'On the mountain,' he said, finally. 'He was sitting there in the snow, looking lost and frightened.'

Turning his gaze to meet Alabaster's, Santa's kind blue eyes were suddenly penetrating and uncharacteristically cold.

'You didn't cross the perimeter, did you?'

'No.' The word came out before Alabaster had chance to stop it. 'Well, not exactly…'

'Not exactly?' Bushy raised an eyebrow.

'I may have gone just a teensy-tiny bit outside the perimeter –'

Bushy growled, his face contorted in rage.

'– but it wasn't my fault. There was an avalanche.'

'And where did you find this creature, Alabaster?' Bushy asked, ignoring the elf's excuses. 'Inside or outside the perimeter?'

Alabaster was rumbled. 'Outside. But I couldn't leave him to die in the cold.'

Alabaster saw Bushy roll his eyes. Bushy was one of Santa's oldest friends and most trusted colleagues, and he made sure everybody else knew it.

It was worth one final effort; Alabaster turned to Santa. 'Can't I keep him? Please?'

Glaring over the top of his half-moon spectacles, Santa looked gobsmacked. Finally, Bushy spoke up:

'Rule number eight hundred and sixty-three, clause fifty-two of the Elf's Handbook firmly states that no pets shall be kept in the grounds of the Grotto. I'm sure I don't need to remind you, Snowball; animals are not to be trusted. They are unpredictable and dangerous, particularly if left to their own devices.'

As if to prove the old elf's point, the little black creature proceeded to take a large chomp out of the topmost sheet of paper on Santa's desk.

'Fluffy, no!' Alabaster cried.

He leapt forward to wrench it from the animal's mouth. Fluffy did not like this one bit, and nipped Alabaster's finger with teeth as sharp as pins. A gob of blood appeared and he winced in pain.

'You've given it a *name*?'

Santa and Bushy exchanged a dark look, followed by a perfectly synchronised shake of their heads.

Fluffy was attempting to pick up the well of ink now. Desperate to prevent any further trouble, Alabaster removed the small bottle from its claws and carefully replaced it back in its holder. He scooped the animal up and placed it gently back into the knapsack that hung from the back of his chair.

After a moment's contemplation, Santa regarded him with narrowed eyes.

'What were you doing on the mountain?'

The little elf wiped his palms on his trousers. 'I was trying out a new invention, sir.'

Bushy Evergreen let out a mirthless snort. 'Yes, when you were *supposed* to have been back at your station, assisting with present-wrapping for the Big Day, not gallivanting about with new-fangled inventions that nobody asked you for.'

Santa gestured for calm with a wave of the hand. Bushy dutifully held his tongue, though with barely-contained indignation still burning on his face.

'This… invention,' Santa said softly. 'Tell me more.'

'Well, sir… it's just a snowboard.'

'*Just* a snowboard?'

Alabaster couldn't help himself. This was his one big chance:

'Not just any snowboard. A *floating* snowboard, enchanted with elf magic.' Alabaster grinned. 'What child on the planet wouldn't love to receive such a gift on Christmas morning?'

Santa looked at him sternly. 'If you take one thing from this conversation, Alabaster, then it is this: humans must never be exposed to magic. Were humans to ever get their hold on elfish magic, their first instinct would be to use it against one another or, worse, against *us.*'

Each word hammered into Alabaster's heart like a rusty nail. Santa was right. Humans could be wretched beings sometimes.

'Besides,' Bushy chimed in, 'you've already demonstrated how easy it is to lose control of a hovering snowboard.'

'It's perfectly easy to control.'

'Then how do you explain arriving back at your station more than three hours late?'

Alabaster cast his gaze downward.

'I don't know, I guess the truth is... I got carried away.'

'Carried away!' Bushy's face was now scarlet, apoplectic with rage. Alabaster imagined steam emitting from his pointy ears. '*Carried away*?! And what if the villagers had seen you up there, on your flying contraption? Did you ever stop to think about that?'

Santa, meanwhile, maintained a calm demeanour, sitting in his chair, watching Alabaster's reaction with patient eyes. Finally, he said,

'Alabaster, some things aren't meant to be. Humans are not to be exposed to our magic, and elves are not permitted to keep pets.' Before Alabaster could protest, Santa continued: 'I understand this is frustrating. But that's just the way it is. Please respect that. Rules exist for a reason.'

Alabaster could feel his emotions rising; his lip began to tremble, and tears threatened to well up behind his eyes. He swallowed hard; he was not going to cry in front of the Big Man. No way.

He managed to say in a hoarse whisper, 'Yes, sir.'

Santa smiled at him. 'You know what you must do.'

Alabaster nodded.

'We will see you back at your station in the morning.'

And with that, Santa lifted his quill from the ink-well and scribbled on a piece of yellowed parchment.

The matter was concluded. The decision had been made: Alabaster would have to return the creature to the snowy wilderness where he had found it.

A feeling of hollowness racked his bones as he lowered himself down from the chair. He lifted the strap of his knapsack over his shoulder and made his way back to the heavy oaken door. From across the room, the shrill voice of Bushy Evergreen scratched at his eardrums:

'At eight-thirty. *Sharp!*'

Four

GOODBYE

As Alabaster trundled up the snow-covered pathway that led away from the twinkling fairy lights of Santa's grotto, a weight sat in the pit of his stomach.

'I'm so sorry, Fluffy.'

He stopped to give the little creature a stroke on the head. In return, it nuzzled against his breast and licked at his cut finger. Alabaster quickly discovered that the gentlest of scratches behind the ears would send one of its hind legs thumping like a mechanical donkey against the inside of the knapsack. He pulled his hand away and gazed at the fat grey snow-clouds gathering above the horizon.

It was all so unfair. The very community that dedicated their lives to making and delivering presents all year round, for some reason, weren't allowed to receive presents themselves. Not even so much as a little pet to provide companionship. Santa's rules sometimes felt like a punishment – one that he had done nothing to earn.

It was a cold evening. A green haze of light stretched and danced across an indigo sky. To keep the creature warm, Alabaster scooped it up and tucked it inside his jumper. With a belly now as large as Bushy Evergreen's, Alabaster trundled through the snow.

Why was Santa so against him keeping the creature, anyway? It wasn't harming anybody. And why couldn't children be given his floating snurfer? If humans really were all that bad, then why did Santa give their offspring treats every year? It made no sense, no sense at all.

Crossing through the Grotto's main gateway, the illuminated houses of the elves' village suddenly disappeared from view. In its place, an enormous blizzard appeared to flurry, as if the Grotto had never existed at all. This was the magic of the Infinity Crystal; the centuries-old charm that kept the Grotto hidden from the prying eyes of the humans, and Santa and the elves safe from intruders.

At the edge of the mountain, Alabaster looked down to see the animal sleeping soundly at his chest. The little thing looked so peaceful, he felt like a wicked elf. But he had no choice.

'Hey,' he crooned at the creature, giving it a nudge. 'You have to wake up now.'

The animal stirred for a moment, slapped its lips and made to go back to sleep.

Alabaster winced. In all of his ninety-four years, this was the hardest thing he had ever done.

He wrapped the sleeping animal in his scarf and placed it on the ground. He took a step backwards. Satisfied that it was asleep, he turned to walk away.

Before he knew it, the cub once again stood before him, its tail wagging with furious excitement.

'No, no – you stay.'

Not understanding, the creature ran between his legs and around his feet. Alabaster tried to walk on, but it followed him.

He would have to be firm.

'Bad Fluffy!' His voice startled the animal, who sat on its haunches, looking frightened. Alabaster built steel bars around his heart, which melted instantly when he detected a tear in the animal's eye. He could not let his emotions cloud his thinking. 'You. Stay. Here.'

Alabaster backed away slowly. This time the animal stayed put. Its cries, however, rose over even the shriek of the persistent blizzard. The creature, wrapped in his scarf, was now only a small orange dot on the landscape, amid a frenzy of whirling snowflakes.

The howling continued.

It was an odd thing: Santa always said you knew you were doing the right thing when you felt a glimmer of pride rise in your heart.

Right now, he felt nothing but shame.

Through blurred vision, Alabaster turned to give Fluffy a final parting glance. Then he spotted it – a brown shadow emerging from the mouth of a cave in the side of the mountain.

A bear.

If the elves of Lapland could be certain of anything, it was that rousing a hibernating bear from its slumber spelled *Very Bad News*.

Oblivious to this wisdom, Fluffy continued to pierce the air with cries like a siren. To make matters worse, the wailing cub was wrapped in Alabaster's bright orange scarf.

The enormous creature now skulked on all fours towards it.

Without pausing to think, Alabaster dropped his knapsack and ran to the cub's protection.

'Fluffy!'

The snow beneath his feet was like a puddle of syrup. Nonetheless, he kept going.

Just at the edge of the trees, the bear reared onto its hind legs and sniffed at the air with its wet black nose.

Food.

It licked its lips and traced a path along the surface

with its nose pressed to the snow, frosts forming a glistening white moustache upon its muzzle. When within arm's length of Alabaster's trembling pet, the bear reared up again and stretched to its full, terrifying size, its claws extended like rows of knives, ready to ensnare its prey in a deadly embrace.

Alabaster reached for the only thing available. He pulled off his snowshoe and flung it with all of his might. The end hit the bear squarely in the eye. The animal howled in pain and anger, exposing a drooling mouth of razor-sharp teeth. In its confusion, Alabaster snatched up the flailing cub and dashed away. Sensing the bear hot on his tail, he turned and pointed the other snowshoe like a sword, ready to throw.

'Don't make me use the other one,' he warned.

The bear grunted, shuffling back and forth warily.

'Go on, get!' Alabaster waved the end of the showshoe in the animal's direction.

The bear snorted as it considered its next move.

'I SAID GET!' Alabaster bellowed, holding on to Fluffy with everything he had.

Finally, the bear turned its head and skulked away, apparently deciding that confronting an angry elf waving a snowshoe was far less appealing than going back to sleep. Once it had retreated to the mouth of its cave, Alabaster lowered the snowshoe and reattached it to the sole of his foot.

He lifted the flap of his satchel and gently placed the creature inside, muttering under his breath all the while. 'You're going to get me into a world of trouble.'

Five

REINDEER MILK

'I hope you like reindeer milk,' Alabaster called from the kitchen, stirring a bubbling saucepan over the stove. 'I don't know what else to offer you. Anyway, a nice cup of reindeer milk is the perfect thing for a good night's sleep.'

The creature, nestled snugly on a cushion in the living room, sniffed the sweet air approvingly.

Alabaster carefully measured out the milk from the saucepan – one half into a Christmas mug, the other half into a cereal bowl – and carried both on a tray. He deposited the tray on the sofa beside his new guest.

'I only have one cup, so I've had to put yours in a bowl, I'm afraid,' Alabaster said with a chuckle. He had never entertained like this before. 'I hope that's ok with you?'

The animal did not seem to mind at all, lapping hungrily at the bowl's steaming contents with a long pink tongue.

All the while, Alabaster continued to chatter incessantly, telling his new guest everything there was to know, in exchange for an occasional confused blink of the creature's huge, black eyes.

It was nice to have someone to talk to.

'They don't sit with me at the canteen,' he was saying. 'I feel like they're avoiding me. It's not my fault I'm a Wild Elf – I was born this way. Sure, I'm a little bigger than the rest of them, and, ok, clumsier, but that doesn't make me a bad elf.

'See, a bad elf would be the sort of elf that just left you out there in the cold. A good elf wouldn't do that.'

Having devoured the portion of reindeer milk, the animal let out a long yawn, and nestled its head on Alabaster's lap.

'The only question is, where are you going to sleep?'

Alabaster glanced around in search of somewhere suitable, then attempted to pick up the creature by the scruff of its neck. As he did so, Fluffy dug its claws into the upholstery. When Alabaster finally succeeded in prizing it off, he almost fainted in horror to see the deep scratch marks that now exposed the cushion's white cotton innards. Each scratch looked like it had been sliced with a cut-throat razor.

Fluffy's claws would need a good clipping if he was to keep his furniture intact.

Tomorrow. It was already getting late.

The cubby-hole under the stairs was probably the best place for now. Alabaster folded a towel for a bed and strung up some fairy lights to make the den feel a little more homely.

With careful hands, he placed the animal on the towel. Then added a cushion. And a bowl to do its business in, in case it woke up in the night.

'Night, little fella,' he soothed as he pulled the door closed. The creature blinked at him, confused. Then it began to cry.

Ignoring the animal's whimpers, Alabaster trundled up to bed.

✿ ✿ ✿

The clock on the bedside table read 11.57. Throughout the house, a shrill, ear-splitting noise honked with the volume and insistence of a car alarm.

'It will have to learn,' Alabaster grunted and pulled a pillow over his ears.

At 12.05, with the din now accompanied by an additional relentless, house-shaking thump, Alabaster relented and trotted gruffly down the stairs. The moment his feet landed in the passageway, the shrieking and banging suddenly stopped. The animal – who, having managed to free itself by smashing through the door with its head – smiled at its owner excitedly and wagged its tail with delight.

'Fluffy, what have you done?!' Alabaster gasped.

From among the debris of broken shards of wood and splinters, the creature let out a playful yowl. It stared at Alabaster dumbly, its long pink tongue lolling at the side.

Summoning all the determination he could not to succumb to anger, Alabaster carried it to his room. He couldn't risk losing any more doors.

'I don't know what we're going to do with you,' he said with a yawn, laying the animal gently on the pillow beside his own. 'Sweet dreams, Fluffy.'

Beside him, the creature dozed happily. Each out-breath carried a shrill wheeze, that sounded in the dark like a party whistle.

He rolled over, pulled the animal towards him and wrapped it in his arms. The wheezing stopped, replaced by a single, long murmur of contentment. The animal's heartbeat thudded against his chest softly as it snored.

Despite everything, the scratched upholstery, the broken doorway, the breath that could strip wall-paint… it was nice to have company.

As long as nobody found out about the creature, there would be no problem.

Finally, with a new pet in his arms, Alabaster drifted off into the most restful sleep he had enjoyed in ages.

Six

THE FACTORY FLOOR

Throughout the month of December, the Grotto factory was, as one might imagine, a frenzy of activity. Every elf in the village, regardless of age or status, was expected to lend their energies to the task of constructing, assembling, painting, packaging and gift-wrapping presents for the world's human children. It was a vast operation, all carried out from start to finish in the factory building, and the elves felt immense pride working under the supervision and guidance of Santa Claus.

Each section of the factory was devoted to its own specialism, with the older, more experienced elves employed in design and construction, where each new item would begin its journey, wending its way through the factory floor along a conveyor belt before finally arriving at the packaging and gift-wrapping section.

Here, Alabaster, along with an army of younger elves, wrapped and decorated each one at a time before depositing them into trolleys piled high with similarly shiny, neatly-wrapped gift-boxes. At this point, the youngest elves (delighted that school took a pause throughout the whole of December) whisked them away on roller skates to the warehouse, ready for distribution on Christmas Day.

Although Alabaster secretly yearned to join the ranks of the inventors and designers at the top of the pecking order, he was often thankful that he was employed in the simple task of gift-wrapping, as it allowed him to daydream to his heart's content. Usually, he spent his time dreaming of some new invention as he folded and taped down the papered edges; today, however, his mind returned to thoughts of another matter altogether: his new lodger.

He hoped the brown sticky tape he had used to temporarily repair the broken cubby-hole door would hold. And that the creature had ceased making the awful mewling noise that greeted his departure for work that morning. At least he could rest assured that Fluffy's racket would not fall on the ears of his neighbours, who were all currently busy at work in the factory.

Suddenly, a chorus of excited whispers shook Alabaster from his reverie, spreading from elf to elf along the production line.

'They're coming.'

'Look lively, elves!'

Sure enough, Santa and Bushy were heading in their direction. They were led by Mary, who was responsible for overseeing the work in the gift-wrapping section. Alabaster dutifully finished off the item he was working on and placed it in the trolley.

'Great work, Alabaster,' Santa said, admiring the elf's freshly-wrapped pile of gifts.

Bushy didn't say anything, but offered a nod, the usual curmudgeonly scowl marking his features.

'Might I make a small suggestion, Alabaster?' said Mary.

'Of course.'

The truth was Alabaster did not mind at all. Mary was one of the nicest elves in the Grotto. She was always the first to greet Alabaster each morning with the sunniest of smiles. It did not matter that she offered the same courtesy to everyone, she made Alabaster feel for a moment as though she and he were the only two elves in Grotto.

'Do you know what would really spruce things up a bit?' Mary's sweet berry perfume wafted under Alabaster's nostrils as she reached across him for a pair of scissors. 'You could give the ribbon an extra little curl by rubbing it against the blade, like this.' She demonstrated the technique as she spoke. When she had finished, the ribbon tails sprang into a pleasing coil. 'Gives it that extra *je ne sais quoi*, don't you think?'

She was right. The gift looked several degrees more pretty.

'You try.'

Alabaster took the scissors and gave the ribbon a sharp tug across the blade. To his disappointment, the fabric sliced in two and fell miserably to the floor.

Mary looked at him sympathetically. 'You'll get the hang of it. It just takes a little practice.'

'With those big, pudgy hands of his?' a voice snickered from above. It belonged to Needles who, along with the other toy-painters, sat perched atop a row of high stools, brushes in hand. Whenever Needles spoke, a pocket of air escaped through a chip in his front tooth, punctuating his words with an involuntary whistle.

'Now, Needles,' Mary chided. 'Everyone has their unique talents and something valuable to contribute...'

'Everyone?' he said, giving Alabaster a derisive smirk.

'Yes, Needles. Everyone.'

Needles let out a snort. 'If you ask me, some jobs aren't meant to be handled by Wild Elves.'

Mary fixed Needles with a stern look. 'No one did ask you, as I recall.' Needles was about to respond but, noting the same expression of disapproval on Mary and Santa's faces, thought better of it and returned to his painting without another word.

'Well, it looks as though you have everything in hand here, Mary,' Santa said, a half-smile teasing the corner of his mouth. 'Well done, team! I think it's time Bushy and I see how they're getting on in the assembly room.' With this, he gave Mary a discreet wink before leading Bushy into the neighbouring section.

Undeterred by Needles's comments, Alabaster collected another boxed item from the conveyor belt and laid it on a large square of wrapping paper. A hand suddenly landed on his shoulder and gave a gentle squeeze.

'Don't pay any attention to him,' Alvin's voice muttered low in his ear. 'The painters always think they're better than everyone else, but it wasn't so long ago they were doing the exact same jobs as the rest of us.'

Alvin, being not one of the brightest elves in the factory, was assigned to box-folding duties.

'They would do well to remember that.'

Alabaster was startled; it was unusual for any of the factory elves to speak to him, let alone touch him.

'I appreciate that, Alvin,' he said, finally. 'Thanks.'

Once Santa and Bushy were out of earshot, Mary summoned everybody's attention.

'Quickly, gather round, team,' she said in a conspiratorial half-whisper. Obligingly, the elves rose from their seats and congregated around Mary's station. 'As you know, tomorrow my uncle will be celebrating a big birthday tomorrow – his seven hundred and fiftieth, no less.'

The assembled elves responded with whistles and gasps, clearly impressed with the elf's grand old age.

'With Christmas preparations in full swing, December birthdays do tend to be overlooked. So I'm pleased to announce that, this year, Santa and I are determined to make it a special one for him. Tomorrow afternoon at three, we're going to have a surprise party in the square. Naturally, everyone is invited.'

While the elves clapped their approval, Mary reached under the table and produced a large white box.

'To mark the occasion, I've made something a bit special. I hope you like it.'

She unboxed the lid and held it up for everybody to see. Inside was a large hand-made cake, bearing a detailed likeness of Bushy Evergreen's face. Every fibre of his beard and bristly eyebrows protruded from the sponge in layers of silvery iced sugar. The room cooed in admiration.

'There's just one problem – as you know, my uncle and I share the same home, so I don't have anywhere safe to store it. What I need is someone to help look after it, just for tonight.'

Before he had even had time to consider it, Alabaster's voice rang out across the factory. 'I'll do it Mary!'

Mary blinked at him in surprise, along with the hundred-or-so other elves in the wrapping section.

'Oh, sure,' Needles laughed. 'It'll be the last we see of it.'

'Needles, that's not nice,' Alvin hissed.

'Come off it. Everyone knows Wild Elves are notorious for being unable to manage their instincts. He'll have gobbled it up before he's set foot outside the building. Why take the risk when there are others available that you already know you can rely on.'

Mary looked unimpressed. 'You, I suppose?'

Needles grinned. 'At your service.'

'That's very kind of you, Needles, but...'

'The pleasure's all mine, truly.'

Mary paused.

'You don't want to entrust such a beautiful thing with someone like him, do you?'

It was all Alabaster could stand. Before he knew it, he let out a roar of frustration that reverberated around the factory like a roll of thunder. When the sound had died, Alabaster looked around, mortified to see that everyone was staring at him.

It was Needles who finally broke the silence.

'See, what did I tell you? Wild Elves are incapable of controlling their emotions.'

'Alabaster, wait,' Mary said. But it was too late.

He was out the door.

The silence that shrouded the room in the wake of Alabaster's departure was broken by Needles, who gave a mirthless chuckle.

Mary glowered at him. 'Needles, why did you do that? That's exactly the sort of behaviour that earns someone a strike on the Naughty List.'

Needles shrugged indignantly. 'No-one ever wound up on the Naughty List for telling the truth.'

Mary scowled. 'They do when they deliberately set out to hurt someone's feelings.'

'It's not my fault some elves can't handle the truth,' he retorted with a petulant shrug.

There was little point in arguing. Mary took up the cake and followed Alabaster.

❄ ❄ ❄

Outside the front entrance to the factory, Alabaster was sitting on a bench. He was staring at the snow on the ground, a cloud of vapour billowing from his flared nostrils.

'Don't pay any attention to him, Alabaster,' said Mary as she sat beside him.

He kept his eyes to the floor. 'It's so frustrating, Mary. No matter what I do... I could be the nicest elf in all the Grotto and they still wouldn't see it. All I am to them is a stupid Wild Elf.'

'Stop talking that way, Alabaster. Do you hear me?'

'Well, it's true,' he muttered.

Mary sighed. 'Did you ever stop to think why Needles is pushing your buttons?' she said finally. 'It's because he's jealous of you.'

Alabaster looked up with incredulity. 'Jealous? Of me?!'

'Of course. The only thing he can do is try to bring you down to his level. Don't let him.'

'But why would he be jealous of me?'

Mary smiled at him. 'A light shines in you, Alabaster Snowball, that Needles will never have. And he knows it. I only wish you did too.'

Alabaster was touched. She was wrong of course, but it was nice she thought so.

'In fact, nothing would give me greater pleasure than if you would look after this.'

She picked up the box and held it to Alabaster. He took it and lifted the lid. Bushy's curmudgeonly likeness glowered up at him.

'It's really beautiful, Mary.' He was only half-lying – the care and attention to detail was truly astonishing. 'It must have taken ages.'

'You have no idea,' she chuckled. 'Listen, if you take this home now, you can take as long as you need. And if

Santa asks, I'll tell him you're running an errand for me.'
She gave a bright smile.

Sometimes it seemed quite impossible to Alabaster that she could have been in any way related to Bushy Evergreen.

'Ok, Mary.'

Alabaster could not help but smile back.

Seven

BUSHY'S BIRTHDAY SURPRISE

The next morning was a Saturday, Alabaster's favourite day of the week. It was also the day of Bushy Evergreen's surprise party.

Having returned a violently reluctant Fluffy to the cubby-hole and resealed it with yesterday's tape, he checked on the cake inside the refrigerator. From the second shelf down, Bushy's likeness scowled up at him. Alabaster smiled.

He made his way to the town square, where Mary was certain to have her hands full with preparations for the party. If she needed an extra pair of hands, he was only too willing to oblige.

When he got there, it seemed everything was under control. A row of candy-cane striped stalls had been erected, offering popcorn, toffee apples and candy-floss, as well as a variety of carnival games.

The Grotto's inhabitants certainly knew how to throw a party!

Between each stall, flags of red and white bunting fluttered in the breeze. Connecting them all was an enormous hand-painted banner which read 'HAPPY BIRTHDAY UNCLE BUSHY' in big colourful letters. Beside it was an ancient black-and-white image of the old elf in his younger days, long before he had grown his great beard and lost his smile. Best of all, and to Alabaster's delight, gently wobbling in the very centre of the square stood a giant inflatable castle.

Despite his ninety-four years, Alabaster felt a profound desire to leap up and try it out before any of the other guests arrived. Elves, unlike humans, retained their sense of fun long into their hundreds. Not that a hundred years was any age at all for an elf, who typically lived to be over a thousand. Provided, of course, that nothing went wrong.

Humans, by comparison, did not live very long at all. If they made it to even a single hundred, it was something of a rarity. What's more, the period known as childhood for a human was devastatingly brief, lasting only something like twelve or thirteen years. Elves, on the other hand, didn't begin to act like teenagers until they had at least reached their hundred and twentieth birthday.

It was all very sad. Perhaps that was the reason Santa felt compelled to reward human children with presents, while they were still young enough to enjoy simple things, before the burdens of adulthood arrived and snatched it all away.

Alabaster circled the town square several times, but Mary was nowhere to be seen. A handful of elves that he knew from the factory were putting the finishing touches to the stall displays, but no-one he knew well.

He was relieved to spot Alvin among them.

'Have you seen Mary?' he asked.

'She's just gone to get some last-minute things,' Alvin said. 'She realised we didn't have quite enough candles for Bushy's cake. And a fire extinguisher. Did you know seven hundred and fifty candles represent a fire risk? I certainly didn't.'

'Oh,' said Alabaster. He was disappointed to have missed her. 'Is there anything you guys need any help with?'

Alvin shook his head with a smile. 'Everything is under control. All that's left for you to do is to go and get ready, and bring the birthday cake before people start arriving.'

'The cake. Right. And when is that?'

'Around three.'

Alabaster looked at his watch. Two hours away, plenty of time.

'Got it.'

And with that, he turned on his heels and returned home.

❀ ❀ ❀

When Alabaster opened his front door, he was horrified to find his living room in a state of disarray. The kitchen bore evidence of a raid; the contents of the cupboards were splashed up the walls, a gloopy concoction of milk, eggs and flour, smeared across the door-frame with the incriminating imprint of a long, pointed tongue. On the floor beneath it sat the cub, its grinning face covered in gunk.

Alabaster was as furious as he was shocked. He fixed the animal with an angry glare and bellowed: 'Bad Fluffy!'

No sooner had the words left his lips than the cub had squatted on its haunches to relieve itself in fear. Alabaster scooped up the leaking animal and dashed to the bathroom. To make matters worse, there was a knock at the door.

'Won't be a minute!'

Once the animal was finally done, Alabaster set it down on the floor and bolted for the door.

'You wait here,' he hissed, and pulled the bathroom door behind him.

Through the peep-hole, Mary's dimpled smile beamed back at him.

There was no way he could let her see the state of the place – it looked an absolute fright.

'Hi, Mary,' he said, opening the door a fraction.

'Hi, Alabaster, sorry to disturb you, mind if I come in?'

Alabaster froze while his mind raced for an excuse. He was rescued by an ear-splitting banging sound that shook the house as the animal butted its head against the inside of the bathroom door. The light fixtures rattled in time with the steady *thump-thump-thump*...

'Now's... not a great time.'

'Is everything ok?'

'Just having some building work done. The house is a bit of a mess...'

'Oh, I really don't mind,' Mary said, and before Alabaster knew what had happened, she was inside the door. A glance into the living room quickly became a double-take. Her nose wrinkled with displeasure. 'Oh, my!'

Alabaster winced. He looked around. It was even worse than he had remembered.

'I just came to collect the *thing* you said you'd look after for me,' Mary said, just above a whisper.

'The thing…?'

Another ear-splitting bang sounded, accompanied by a crack. Fluffy seemed intent on breaking the very rafters of his house.

Mary cupped her mouth with her hands, even though there was nobody around to hear. 'The *thing…* for my uncle?'

The cake! Of course.

'Yes. I'll go get it. Won't be a moment.'

Leaving Mary with an awkward smile, Alabaster scuttled to the kitchen, careful not to step in the mess that lay all about the floor.

'Goodness me, what a racket they're making,' Mary said, the incessant pounding from the bathroom growing ever louder.

'They've been at it all week,' Alabaster called from the kitchen. 'Hopefully it won't be much longer now.'

He opened the refrigerator and his heart fell through the floor. On the second shelf where the cake had been, there now stood half-a-cake. Where it hadn't been chomped into, it bore the indentations of deeply-embedded hoof-prints. A miserable gloop of icing flopped over the edge of the stand.

Mary pinched her nostrils. 'And just what is that dreadful smell?'

'Uh, Mary,' Alabaster stammered. 'There's been a bit of an accident…'

'An accident?'

With a grimace, he held up the remains of the cake. The colour drained from Mary's cheeks. The animal's mewling and butting continued all the while.

Alabaster wanted to apologise, say something, anything, to rescue the situation, but Mary was the first to speak.

'I trusted you.' Her eyes brimmed with tears as she turned on her heels and tore out the door. 'Needles was right about you all along, Alabaster Snowball! How could you!'

'Mary, wait; I can explain…!'

But there was nothing he could do except watch Mary disappear up the road, her sobbing face in her hands.

A large clump of soggy icing dropped from the edge of the stand and landed on the kitchen floor with a plop.

When Alabaster opened the bathroom door, the cub smiled up at him and leapt into his arms, giving his face a big lick with its enormous tongue.

Fixing the animal with a scowl, he grumbled, 'We're going to have to build you a cage.'

Eight

THE NAUGHTY LIST

Alabaster did not attend the party.

He spent the evening building a solid steel cage. The following day, after a sleepless night, he decided to make an enormous replacement cake for Mary. Though it didn't quite bear the same resemblance to Bushy, Alabaster nonetheless arranged to have it delivered to Mary at the factory the next working day. Its arrival, however, seemed to make her more furious than ever and – shooting him a withering glare from across the factory floor – she returned the item to the delivery elf.

Alabaster's heart shattered into a million pieces.

It did nothing to help Alabaster's nerves when Bushy Evergreen's voice rattled over the tannoy: 'Alabaster

Snowball, please report to Santa's office – *immediately!'*

Alabaster set down a half-wrapped item and made his way to the large oaken door of Santa's office, a knot tightening in his stomach. His fist hovered tentatively over its shiny brown surface. After a moment's pause, he knocked.

A gruff voice bellowed, 'Come in.'

Steadying his nerves, Alabaster pushed open the heavy door to see Santa at his desk, reading a broadsheet newspaper that obscured his entire body.

'Please, take a seat.' A hand emerged from one side of the newspaper and gestured towards the chair opposite.

Alabaster obliged. His legs trembled back and forth involuntarily as he waited to find out what new trouble he was in.

Had Fluffy been discovered? Perhaps his neighbours had raised complaints about the strange noises. Perhaps the chemist had raised the alarm about his peculiar purchase of one hundred nappies.

He could bear the silence no longer.

'What is this about, Santa?'

Santa lowered the paper. He laid the newspaper flat on the desk, and turned his gaze to the window.

'Am I a bad person, Alabaster?' he asked, finally.

Alabaster wondered whether this was some kind of trick question, but Santa's rueful expression showed it was meant with utmost sincerity.

'Of… of course not,' Alabaster stammered. 'You're Santa – the most beloved person in the history of… of everything!'

Santa looked down. 'That's what I used to believe.'

Alabaster tilted the newspaper so that he could read the front page. The little elf could barely believe his eyes.

The headline read: 'Santa's Secret Agenda: The Dark Side of Christmas – Wilhelmina Turnpike investigates'.

'What is this?'

'Read it.'

Alabaster read:

For centuries, he has been regarded as the jolly old gift-giver who, once a year, brings joy and happiness to children across the globe. However, with recent studies indicating a significant decline in children's behaviour and attitudes, it is time we ask ourselves the question: Is Santa to blame?

When children are rewarded for bad behaviour, studies show, their behaviour deteriorates. Awarding presents willy-nilly to children that have done nothing to deserve them is a recipe for disaster and social decay.

Which begs the question: just what is the driving force behind Santa's bizarre scheme to shower children with gifts? For years, we have assumed that it is all down to some innocent (if

misplaced) desire to spread benevolence and joy –
but what if it isn't?

What if Santa's driving force is something
much darker?

Over the next few weeks, we will be
investigating the motivations behind the
merriment and find out once and for all whether,
as some have suggested, Santa is, in fact, trying to
buy our children's loyalty. Does he mean to take
control of their minds as part of some sinister
plot?

We will be conducting interviews with
psychologists, fellow toy manufacturers and
former employees to get to the truth – and discover
once and for all the real cost of Christmas.

Alabaster dropped the newspaper onto Santa's desk
as if the sheets themselves were laced with poison. 'But
this… this is outrageous,' he stammered. 'Hysterical
hogwash!'

'I agree,' Santa said. 'Which is why I am giving you
this.'

He opened a drawer from underneath his desk and
pulled out a long mahogany box. He passed it across
the table.

Alabaster gazed with intense curiosity.

'Open it.'

Alabaster lifted the lid. Inside, on a bed of straw, there lay a tightly-rolled scroll of yellow parchment.

'What is it?'

'Open it up.'

Alabaster unpicked the seal and unrolled it, revealing a long column of hundreds of names in brilliant gold script.

'This,' Santa said in a hushed tone, 'is the Naughty List.'

Alabaster gazed at the parchment. The text upon it was moving! The letters shifted around on the page as new words and names appeared. Beside each name was a list all of their misdemeanours.

'I have long needed someone to do this job for me and, Alabaster, I think you are just the elf.'

Alabaster stared in amazement as he skimmed the scroll's ever-changing contents, a slew of new additions appearing before his very eyes.

'What do you need me to do?'

'It's a big job – this list includes not only children the world over but their adults as well, and includes misdemeanours going back to the day they were born. I need you to go through it all with a fine tooth-comb and note the names of children whose behaviour in the past year means they should not be rewarded with presents.'

Alabaster stared in wide-eyed amazement. He could not believe what he was seeing.

'It would be an honour,' he said as he turned his eyes back to Santa's. He wrapped up the scroll and placed it back in its box.

'You'll be doing me a great service, Alabaster,' he said, a warm smile brightening his face. 'I won't forget this.'

With a nervous chuckle, Alabaster left Santa's office and returned to his workstation. There, he unrolled the parchment again, to make sure his eyes weren't deceiving him.

They were not.

Near the bottom, nestled among the Snodgrasses, Snoebergers, Snoswells and Snotts flashed his own name: Alabaster Snowball.

Nine

THE KRAMPUS GOES MISSING

As soon as Alabaster got home he prised open the lid of the mahogany box and laid the naughty list flat on the table. He gazed in bewilderment at the ever-changing text.

Alabaster wondered if the parchment might run out of room for more names. However, no matter how much it seemed he was close to the end of the scroll, there was always more.

By the light of the golden glow that shrouded the unravelled scroll, he read. The name of one *Charlie Adams (8)* appeared near the top, alongside his geographical location – *Knightsbridge, London* – and his misdemeanour: *Pulling Billy Samson (7)'s hair. Blaming Dominic Brown (3).*

There were many others:

* *Jessica Hughes (8) – Birkenhead, Liverpool – stealing fifty pence left by the tooth fairy under her brother's pillow. Lying about it to Mum and Dad.*
* *Floyd Morgan (12) – Dundee, Scotland – Lying to Mum and Dad about his score in his English test. Forging Mum's signature.*
* *Simon Rivers (9) – Ashford, Kent – Breaking Mrs Ashton (76)'s front window with a football. Blaming Tessa Donahue (7).*

Hundreds of similar offences poured down the length of the apparently bottomless scroll. Alabaster frowned. It was certainly going to take a lot of work to keep on top of all of these naughty children.

And there, near the bottom, amongst the ever-growing list of names, was his own:

Name: Alabaster Snowball;
Region: Lapland;
Misdemeanour: venturing beyond the Elfland boundary; defying Santa's instructions; taking in the krampus cub as a pet; lying to Santa.

Krampus?

So that was what the creature was called.

Hopefully this was the only list of its kind. If Bushy saw this he would be in *big trouble*.

He looked up at the clock. Five forty-five. Usually at this time of day he would be famished. However, the worry of seeing his own name on Santa's Naughty List had stifled his appetite somewhat.

Nevertheless, it was Fluffy's feeding time.

In the kitchen, the window had been left open, and the thin net curtains that covered it fluttered softly from the evening breeze outside. It was little wonder the house felt so chilly.

He heated up two portions of lasagne, one for himself and one for Fluffy. It was a relief having a house that felt calm and quiet again after the chaos of the past few days. The cage he had built for the krampus was clearly achieving its intended purpose and keeping the animal under control.

After he had plated up the meals, he went to the alcove under the stairs to give the creature its food.

'I hope you're hungry,' he called, imagining its tail suddenly sweeping with excitement at the sound of his voice. 'There's enough here to feed a wolf!'

He rounded the corner into the passageway and turned on the light.

The cubby-hole door was ajar. He was certain he had

locked it before leaving that morning.

The silence of the house at once no longer felt calm and peaceful, but ominous and dark. Dread and nausea rose in Alabaster's tummy. He could hardly bear to look inside.

When he pulled open the door, his worst fears were confirmed.

Fluffy was gone.

Ten

FINDING FLUFFY

Where the cage's narrow metal bars had once stood in even columns, sharp metallic prongs now sprang outwards, as though something inside had exploded.

The caging had been gnawed through.

'Fluffy!'

Alabaster's distress rattled through the house as he ran up and down the stairs in panic.

'Fluffy, where are you?'

He searched everywhere: the bathroom, the closet, under the bed, behind every set of curtains in the house, the basement, the drum of the washing machine, but the creature was nowhere to be found.

He got to his feet and paced while the cogs in his

head continued to spin.

What if it had got stuck somewhere in the cold? What if – Alabaster could barely bring himself to entertain the notion, it was too terrible to contemplate…

What if it had ventured outside of the compound?

Fluffy couldn't know about the Infinity Crystal's magical dome. He would never find his way back in by himself; all he would see was that the Grotto had suddenly vanished into thin air.

And then what? Freeze to death, in all probability. Or, worse, be devoured by a hungry bear, or a wolf, or a human, or any manner of predators that lived beyond the safety of the perimeter.

After investigating all of the little house's nooks and crannies, Alabaster returned to the kitchen and the window that had been left open. The snow-coated window-pane bore little indentations… hoof-prints.

Alabaster's heartbeat thudded in his ears as he bolted out the front door into the garden. A thin trail of prints disappeared into the row of hedges that separated his garden from his neighbour's.

'Fluffy!' he called, his voice low enough not to alert the neighbours to anything untoward, but hopefully loud enough that the creature might hear.

A light shower of snow was beginning to fall. If he was going to follow the trail, he would have to be quick.

Tracks of parallel prints led into the next garden,

and the one after that, until they led to the open clearing of the main road where it was intersected by the tracks of husky-drawn sleds.

It was hopeless. The creature could be anywhere by now.

'Fluffy!' he called. 'Fluffy!'

The downpour of snow grew thicker with every minute and the krampus's prints were beginning to vanish. Alabaster traced them as far as he could before the thickening snow wiped away any trace. To his horror, it appeared that they were headed directly out of the Grotto's main entrance, beyond the walls of the invisibility dome.

Alabaster's heart sank into his stomach.

There was nothing for it but to return home, tired and anxious, and hope upon hope that the krampus had somehow got there before him.

✿ ✿ ✿

Back home there was no sign of the animal. Not a footprint, not a hair.

Poised at the edge of the sofa, chewing at the last of his fingernails, Alabaster thought of every possible scenario, each one worse than the last.

What if it had been caught along the way? Would Santa find out? And if he did, wouldn't it be obvious who was to blame, seeing as it was Alabaster himself who brought the creature to Santa's office only a week ago?

The feeling of helplessness was intolerable, the not-knowing whether it was better to stay put and wait, or venture out again and make another attempt at scouring the village.

Worst of all was having nobody to tell. There was not a single person he could confide in without dire consequences. Sugarplum Mary, maybe... but given the past couple of days, he didn't hold much hope for being on her Christmas card list this year.

He sat on the sofa for another agonising hour. Then another. And another. By the time the clock struck four, it was long past his bedtime. Nonetheless, he remained wide awake, pulling back the curtains every few minutes in the hope of any sign that the animal might have found its way home.

There was none.

The snow had since stopped, and the road outside was calm and quiet. All the neighbouring houses stood in darkness while the village slept.

Alabaster could no longer bear doing nothing.

While waiting, an idea occurred to him. If the krampus had ventured out of the compound, then he had to help it find its way home, even if that meant making the Grotto temporarily visible.

It was risky, certainly. But he had to do something. At this time of morning, there would be nobody around to see him.

Nobody need ever know.

From a large sweet tin kept on top of the kitchen cupboard, Alabaster refilled his pouch with levitation powder. From the closet, he retrieved the haversack containing the snurfer. Then finally, he pulled on his coat and scarf for the last time and went outside.

Eleven

THE INFINITY CRYSTAL

According to legend, the Infinity Crystal was housed within Santa's office, behind a secret entrance. Once, when an emergency blockage in the gift-wrapping machinery had required Alabaster to make an unscheduled visit to Santa's office, he could have sworn he had seen out of the corner of his eye Shinny Upatree appear from behind a revolving bookcase. Though he had pretended that nothing had happened, the old elf had ever since regarded Alabaster with a peculiar look that betrayed the existence of an unspoken secret shared between them.

That had to be where it was kept.

There was only one entrance to the building, standing silent and eerie in the early morning glow of the northern lights, and that was the front door. He would have to place his hand against the ice-pane, and his presence would be recorded. If any questions arose, he could simply tell them he had arrived early to do some additional work. However, knowing Bushy Evergreen, there would be lots of questions on top of questions, and he already had one lie to keep track of.

That was the thing about having to keep a secret, Alabaster was beginning to realise – it meant sometimes having to lie. And the thing about telling a lie was that it raised questions, and each question required another lie, and another, and another, until it grew and grew and grew, much like a snowball.

No, he would have to find another way that would not arouse any further questions.

Taking the snurfer from his haversack, he sprinkled its underside with levitation powder from his pouch, before tossing it right-side-up onto the snow. Alabaster took hold of the rope and pushed forward with his foot. The board began to rise and he steered himself upwards in gentle circles until he was on the roof.

A long metal pole that you could be forgiven for thinking was a lightning rod protruded from the building's spire, reaching ten metres into the sky. It was from the tip of this rod that the enchanted force-field emanated, encapsulating the whole village, shielding the world from the prying eyes of outsiders.

That, in all likelihood, now included the krampus.

He had no other choice. He perched himself on the lip of the chimney and tucked the snurfer back inside his haversack before easing himself down, his back against one side of the wall, his feet pressed against the other.

It was a lot harder than he had imagined. And a lot dirtier. When he emerged in the fireplace several minutes later, he was covered in soot.

Alabaster dusted himself off as well as he could so as not to leave any trace on the carpet. He removed his blackened shoes and left them inside the grate.

In the darkness of the office, the edges of Santa's desk were barely visible. Perhaps it was a trick of the light, but the eyes on the portraits above Santa's desk seemed to frown upon Alabaster, their judgemental gaze following him around the room.

A twinge of guilt pricked at Alabaster's conscience. First a secret, then a lie… now breaking and entering?

It was astonishing how quickly it had all snowballed.

A wooden cuckoo clock suddenly rang out, and Alabaster just about leapt out of his skin. Five cuckoos. It wouldn't be very long until the first elves began to arrive for their morning shift. He would have to hurry.

Shuffling along the carpeted floor so as not to stub his toes on any hidden corners, he came to a small bookcase. He tiptoed along each of the shelves, tilting fistfuls of books towards himself in the hope that one of them would trigger the mechanism. Finally, he got to one that felt like a hollow block of wood, and pulled it forward.

Suddenly, the bookcase and the semicircle of carpet around it spun around and whisked him into another room.

Alabaster gasped in amazement.

The stone chamber was completely dark, but for a single ball of bright white-blue light, which hovered halfway between the points of two enormous steel icicles, one stretching up from the ground and the other reaching down from the ceiling. An ethereal, high-pitched hum seemed to come directly from the glowing ball of crystal.

Alabaster gulped heavily and tiptoed closer, the cold of the stone floor penetrating the soles of his damp socks. It was just out of reach, even on tip-toes. So, as before, he took out the snurfer from his haversack and steered himself upwards.

He hovered for a moment, gazing at the glowing, suspended crystal. It was the size of a tennis ball, with the texture of a cut-glass diamond.

He knew what he was doing was wrong. But was it really that bad to do something wrong in order to prevent something even worse from happening? If taking the crystal meant that he was saving a life, then surely the taking of the crystal wasn't such a bad thing at all.

At least, that was the thought in his head when he reached out.

At the touch of his pudgy elvish fingers, the hum died, along with the brilliant white-blue light, leaving only darkness. He waited for an alarm, but none came. There was just deathly silence.

Holding the crystal carefully in both hands, Alabaster steered himself back to the ground where a square sliver of thin light indicated the location of the bookcase. In the darkness, he felt along the length of the shelf until he once again found the book that would rotate the bookcase to its original position.

When he succeeded, he half-expected to find himself surrounded by Santa, Bushy Evergreen and a legion of angry elves demanding an explanation for his actions. But the room was empty.

There was only one thing for it, and that was to return home as quickly as possible and see if his strategy had worked. He quickly pulled on his shoes and levitated back up the way he had come, up through the chimney and back towards home.

Twelve

ANOTHER FIVE MINUTES

Amid the gloom of the sunless December morning, the lights of the village began to ignite; the first tell-tale signs of the villagers rising to meet the day. Pots of tea made from berries and nettles harvested back in the summer brewed over open stoves. While the streets remained empty, Alabaster circled the area a few more times, before finally giving up his search and guiding the floating snurfer towards his front door.

He gazed up at the atmosphere. To his great relief, nothing appeared out of the ordinary. Perhaps the view of the stars, vast, bright and infinite seemed a little clearer to the eye, but that could just as easily have been a figment of his troubled conscience. To anyone that did not know the truth, it would appear just the same as any ordinary day.

In his pocket, the crystal orb seemed to weigh more heavily than ever.

A small corner of his mind still entertained the hope that the cub would be sitting on the front doorstep when he arrived. He felt a pang of disappointment when he arrived at his doorstep and confirmed this wasn't the case.

How long it might take for the cub to return wasn't a question he had considered. Maybe never. Nor, indeed, how long he should be prepared to keep the crystal in his possession. He told himself a day. Two at the very most. Three, absolute tops.

Luckily for Alabaster, he did not have to wait long.

No sooner had he set foot in the door than he was almost knocked off his feet by the force of the little creature throwing itself at the elf with all of its might.

'Fluffy! You came back!'

The little animal's tail swung back and forth with excitement as it licked at Alabaster's face with its pink, pointed tongue. In the short time he had taken responsibility for the cub, it had grown even larger. The nubbins that had begun to emerge from its head were beginning to take the shape of rather sharper horns which, each time it leapt at him, bore painfully into the soft fleshy part beneath Alabaster's chin.

'Easy, now,' Alabaster crooned, 'take it easy.'

He carried it to the sofa and sat it on his lap. After a few minutes of calming the animal with gentle strokes along its wiry coat, it began to sleep soundly.

The crystal. Now that the creature had come back, he needed to return the crystal to its rightful place. Immediately. Before Santa and the others got there.

The krampus snored softly in his lap, whimpering intermittently as its emerging horns scratched softly against Alabaster's belly.

He didn't have the heart to disturb the animal's slumber.

Five more minutes, he told himself. Besides, he deserved a little rest before going back out and facing the cold.

And with that thought, Alabaster closed his eyes and fell fast asleep.

Thirteen

NOBODY NEEDS TO KNOW

When Alabaster opened his eyes, Fluffy was still fast asleep on his lap. He squinted at the clock above the fireplace. It read eleven-fifty-four!

At once, he dove into the bathroom, brushed his teeth, combed his hair – which, not having had time to take a shower, refused to be tamed – threw on his work clothes, locked the krampus in the cubby-hole under the stairs, and bolted out the front door.

With knees of jelly, he sprinted to the Grotto with all the energy he could muster, thoughts of what he might say to excuse his lateness – and the trouble he would be in – at the forefront of his mind.

The crystal in his pocket bounced against his thigh as he ran. He would have to return it, of course, as soon as he possibly could. The trouble now was getting into Santa's office without being seen, a task that would be nigh impossible under the beady gaze of Bushy Evergreen, in broad twilight.

Finally, he skidded up the pathway to the factory, placed his palm on the ice monitor and passed through the sliding doors.

Bushy Evergreen was waiting in the lobby, his face stern. Alabaster winced in anticipation of the telling-off he was about to receive… but it never came. The old elf did not even raise an eyebrow as Alabaster skirted past him, up the red-carpeted stairs and into the factory.

With some relief, Alabaster ducked through the double-doors and into his gift-wrapping station. Around him, everything carried on as normal: elves busily wrapping and cutting and sticking the next slew of presents that rounded the conveyor belt. Now that it was the fifteenth of December, it was fast approaching Christmas, their busiest time of year. Perhaps his absence had not even been noticed. He prayed that this was the case.

He dropped his bag under his desk and was about to get straight to work when Mary approached.

If anyone would know of the situation, she would.

'Morning, Mary,' he said, giving his best impression

of an innocent smile. As soon as he spoke, she stopped in her tracks, a confused look on her face. Then, without saying a word, she retreated and made her way back to her own station.

How very odd.

Perhaps she had still not forgiven him for the cake incident. He would have to make amends somehow.

Frowning, Alabaster turned his attention to the items that were making their way around the carousel. He rolled back his sleeves and readied himself to begin the task of wrapping them. He took the first, wrapped it quickly and placed it on the conveyor belt, then another and another.

He wondered if Santa was even inside his office. If he wasn't, maybe he could sneak in, return the crystal and then creep back out again without being detected.

The thin pane of glass beside the door did not betray any movement from within.

It was a huge risk. Perhaps it would be better to wait until nightfall when nobody was around. But then, the longer the Grotto was left visible, the more vulnerable it remained.

Placing the next item on the conveyor belt, he noticed from the corner of his eye a thick black smudge on his work outfit. The soot from the chimney! He had been in such a daze while rushing to work, he had not noticed the state of his tunic.

How on earth was he going to explain this?

At that moment, the sound of approaching voices grew louder.

It was Kringle and Crackerjack, the factory foremen.

He was about to utter the words, 'I can explain' when one of them exclaimed, 'Still not here.' Then the two elves exchanged shrugs, turned on their heels and walked away.

Alabaster stood open-mouthed. What on earth was going on?

Then it dawned on him.

He was *invisible*.

Fourteen

A VERY PRIVATE MEETING

Of course!

The crystal in his pocket was still working its magic – but on him!

Best of all, invisibility gave him the perfect opportunity to return the crystal to the security room without being detected.

He crouched behind Santa's office and pressed an ear to the door. On the other side, Santa's low voice rumbled, punctuated intermittently with the snarky, clipped tones of Bushy Evergreen. There was also another voice Alabaster did not recognise. It was a shame the door muffled everything they were saying; it sounded as though there was an argument going on.

But, then again... what was there to stop him going in?

Twisting the handle gently, Alabaster let himself into Santa's office and closed the door behind him without a sound. Bushy Evergreen twitched for a moment and glared in his direction, before returning his attention to the animated discussion between Santa and the person sitting opposite.

The stranger faced away from Alabaster. From behind it looked human. It had thinning black hair, which Alabaster assumed was usually kept underneath the tall top hat that sat on the chair beside him.

'But you can't,' Santa was saying.

'On the contrary, my friend,' the stranger said, 'I think you'll find it is *you* who can't.' He deposited a sheet of paper onto Santa's desk with a thud. 'Section seven of ordinance nine-B specifically states planning permission be necessary for the building of properties for the purposes of construction and distribution.'

Alabaster had no idea what the words meant, but they sounded very serious, and the human's manner very official.

'Unless you can produce documentary evidence by midnight tonight, I'm afraid ownership of these premises automatically returns to the rightful owner.'

Santa shifted uncomfortably in his chair. 'And who might that be?'

'You're looking at him.'

Alabaster felt a cold chill run through his body. What on earth was happening?

'Think about what you're doing,' Santa stammered. 'All the children…'

The man got up.

'Midnight, Mr Claus.'

He picked up his hat and swept out the door, his long, black velvet cape swishing behind him.

Fifteen

THE AFTERMATH

After the stranger's departure, Santa stared agape at the document left behind. Then he buried his face in the palms of his hands. Bushy Evergreen stood awkwardly beside him, unsure of how best to respond. The old elf was not renowned for his empathy skills.

Finally, Santa broke the silence. 'How could this have happened, Bushy?'

'I… I'm afraid I don't know.'

'How did he get in?'

For the first time in Alabaster's ninety-four year old memory, the old man looked at a loss for words.

'We can't let this happen, Bushy. Is there nothing we can do?'

'If we are unable to provide the document…'

'There is no document. We were here long before the humans arrived. How were we to know of their ordinances and regulations?'

Santa looked as though he were on the brink of tears, his usually rosy cheeks now pale with anguish.

Bushy looked at the floor.

'But now… somehow… they've found us.'

They sat in solemn silence for what seemed like an eternity, until Santa finally stood up and put on his coat.

'Wh-where are you going?' stammered Bushy.

Santa paused at the door, a frown darkening his features. 'Some fresh air would do me good, my friend. I need time to think.'

And with that he was gone.

For a moment, Bushy sat in perfect stillness. Then he found himself beginning to weep.

'This is bad,' he sniffled to himself, 'so very… very bad.'

He paced back and forth several times, stopping occasionally to read and re-read the document, then paced again. Finally, he followed in Santa's footsteps and slammed the door behind him.

Alabaster was alone.

This was all his fault.

Worst of all, however much he racked his brain for a solution, he had to concede there was now nothing that could be done to rectify the situation. Even returning the crystal to its rightful place would not undo the stranger's arrival.

Nonetheless, while the coast was clear, Alabaster did what he had come to do. After letting himself through the secret bookcase, he hovered up to the point where the two enormous icicles met and deposited the crystal. There was an enormous flash of electric blue light as the magic once again resumed its power and Alabaster – now fully visible – returned the way he had come.

Sixteen

CORNELIUS BANDERSNATCH

By lunchtime a spark of gossip circulated until it engulfed the factory like wildfire.

'It's true, I tell you: a human… in the Grotto!'

'I heard he has a head the shape of a boiled egg!' said one.

'His cape is as dark as a human heart!'

'Well, upon my word!'

'What could he want with us?'

With a grim sense of foreboding, the elves continued with their usual work, albeit less cheerfully and focused than normal. Their curiosity was finally answered in the early afternoon, when an unfamiliar voice rang out over the tannoy.

'Good morning, elves,' it said. 'Your presence is required at the main hall.'

Exchanging looks of concern, the elves retired their work tools and made their way to the meeting point in near silence. Once there, their low voices grew into an anxious hum. Alabaster positioned himself near the back of the congregation, barely able to bring himself to witness what was about to unfold.

First, Bushy Evergreen plodded nervously to the centre of the stage. He stood for a moment and cleared his throat.

'Brothers and sisters,' he began. He surveyed the crowd, an anguished expression tightening his lips, then took a deep breath. 'We have called you here because, as you may have heard, there have been some developments in the past few days.'

The murmur of the crowd grew louder, and a voice called, 'What is it, Bushy?'

Heaving a shaky sigh, Bushy closed his eyes and tilted his head to one side then the other before speaking again. 'The Grotto has a visitor.'

A deafening silence gave way to intense chatter. Yet more voices rang out above the din:

'What's going on, Bushy?'

'Tell us!'

Bushy raised a hand, and the rumbling of voices gradually subsided.

'He has requested an audience with you.' At this, he lowered his gaze. 'In accordance with his wishes, without further ado, here is our visitor to explain more.'

A hush descended upon the room as the gangly stranger's polished black shoes tapped across the wooden floorboards to the centre of the stage. He seized the megaphone from Bushy's hands and stood for a moment, observing the crowd of expectant onlookers, a curious smirk on his lips, his eyes burning with riveting fire.

'Elves, elvettes and elflings,' he began, punctuating each word with a courteous nod of the head. 'My name is Cornelius. Cornelius Bandersnatch. I speak to you today in the spirit of friendship, and hope that you will receive this day's news with gratitude for the opportunity that my arrival affords you. Each and every single one of you.'

He spoke slowly and measuredly, exuding confidence and a beguiling charm. Alabaster noticed that the elves were already letting down their guard; once-folded arms now hung limply at waists, and mouths that had only moments ago been tightly pursed now hung agog.

'My friends,' he continued, 'it gives me no pleasure to reveal to you all that, until today, you have been strung along a wayward path. I have no doubt it will come as a surprise to you all that the enterprise in which you have found employment has been – in both the spirit and the letter of the law – *illegal.*'

A gasp rose up from the crowd, followed by a chorus of questions and chattering. Cornelius waited, unflinching and serious, until the cacophony once again died down. His dark eyes flickered across the sea of gobsmacked faces.

'You see, this institution, for centuries, has been operating without a legitimate permit of authorisation. Indeed, the very construction of this Grotto was conducted without any agreement or validation from the necessary channels.'

'Where is Santa?' a voice demanded.

At this, the pale stranger licked his lips and closed his eyes officiously.

'I am afraid Santa is otherwise disposed this morning. He is going to be very busy, as he is currently dealing with the legal affairs team responsible for such matters.'

'But surely there must be some mistake,' another ventured. 'There must be something we can do...'

'As of this moment, I am afraid there is nothing that can be done. The premises are currently being seized by the proper authorities, and all manufacturing on the property must, as of this moment, cease and desist.'

After a moment of shocked silence individual voices rang out, breaking the stillness.

'But… whatever will become of us?'

'I have a family of hungry mouths to feed!'

'What will we do now?'

Just ahead of him, Mary stood in a state of shock, her fist pressed to her mouth. Cornelius Bandersnatch held up a hand for calm.

'I would like to assure you that nobody holds a single elf here responsible for this outcome. We recognise it is not your fault that your employer has failed to share this incriminating information with you. It is also not your fault that Santa has been conducting his operation in clear breach of the law for so long – we agree entirely; it is deeply unfair, and very regretful, that you should now have to bear the consequences of the conduct of a criminal mastermind like Mr Claus. However, this is how the situation stands. I am sorry that it is beyond anybody's control. The law is the law, and that is all that remains to be said on the matter.'

He turned, and made as if to leave the stage. Then he stopped, and turned back to face the audience.

'Unless…'

He stood motionless, looking pensive for a moment as he stroked his long chin. The legion of elves before him waited for him to speak in rapt silence.

'There may be a way to resolve this unfortunate situation, after all,' he mused. 'One that won't leave a single elf out of pocket, or having to worry about how they will feed their family, now that the entire community is, for all practical purposes, unemployed.'

A hundred hands shot up at once.

'What is it?'

'Please tell us!'

'What can we do?'

Cornelius smiled. 'Come and work for me.'

Seventeen

THE ELVES DECIDE

'But we can't!'

Back at the workshop, Alabaster climbed onto the motionless conveyor belt to summon the others' attention.

'Santa's given us everything. We can't abandon him.'

Before he knew it, Alabaster was leading an impromptu meeting.

'What other choice do we have, Alabaster?' Alvin said sadly. 'Like the man said, the whole village is going to be closed down. Where else are we going to live?'

The others muttered in agreement. Alabaster felt his cheeks getting hotter as he became more desperate to turn the situation around.

'Mary,' he pleaded. If anyone was going to stand by Santa's side, it would be her. 'You're not going to just up and leave, are you?'

Mary, embarrassed by the weight of the attention now fixed upon her, shifted uncomfortably. 'I don't know, Alabaster,' she said. 'Today has come as a shock.'

'But Santa has been our protector and guardian since... forever. Without Santa discovering me as an orphan, and taking me in, I wouldn't be where I am right now. I can't abandon him. I'm not alone here – Crackerjack, when you needed a place to stay, who took you in, gave you a job and made you part of a community? Come on, guys; are we just going to abandon him?'

Crackerjack shot him a withering look. 'If he had told me I was going to be part of an illegal operation, I would never have accepted!' He turned up his chin with indignation. 'We're lucky we're not being arrested right now.'

A chorus of anger rose from the assembled group. Alabaster shook his head in despair.

Suddenly, a single loud roar pierced through the cacophony of noise: 'QUIET!'

The crowd fell silent. It was Bushy Evergreen.

The sea of elves parted as he made his way towards the conveyor belt. He heaved himself up and stood alongside Alabaster, then eyed the assembled throng with anger.

'Shame on you,' he said. '*All* of you!'

The crowd fell silent.

'When a man makes it his life's mission to keep us all well-cared for, the least we owe is our loyalty. Now, I've no doubt that a shiny, new opportunity by a charming stranger might seem an attractive prospect, but look at what we've got here. Look at what you're throwing away.'

Alabaster regarded him with reluctant admiration, and some relief. For the first time in his life, Alabaster felt a comradeship with the old elf.

'But Bushy,' another elf ventured, 'he has offered us a bigger salary, a bigger home...'

'I've always wanted to see London!' piped up another.

Bushy scowled, his face turning purple with barely-contained fury.

'Do as you please. I, for one, am staying put.' As if to emphasise the point, he sat cross-legged on the floor, his arms folded across his chest, a withering expression on his wrinkled old face. 'Who's with me?'

For what seemed like an eternity, nobody moved. Finally, Alabaster summoned the courage to sit beside him.

Alvin approached the conveyor belt. 'I'm sorry, Bushy,' he said, his low voice racked with regret. 'What Cornelius is offering us is better than being out of a job. We still get to make children happy, and we get to see what it's really like out there in the big, wide world. I'm sorry but... it's not as if we have much of a choice.'

And with that, he walked up through the parted crowd and headed out the door. One by one, others followed suit, shuffling sadly out of the workshop until Alabaster and Bushy were left alone.

'What are you going to do, Alabaster?'

Alabaster stared mournfully down at the feet that now dangled over the conveyor belt's edge.

'I don't know,' he said.

'One thing's for certain,' Bushy said, with a note of resignation that wounded Alabaster's heart, 'nothing will ever be the same again.'

❀ ❀ ❀

That night, Alabaster endured a dreadful night's sleep. No matter how he turned and tossed, he could not put his mind at rest. After turning his pillow over to the cold side for the umpteenth time, he tossed the blanket away. In a few minutes, coldness and discomfort forced him to retrieve it once again. Beside him, the krampus cub snored and snuggled against him, blissfully oblivious to Alabaster's turmoil.

Alabaster did not even notice the pungent fart the krampus emitted as he pressed its belly against his own, squeezing it like a teddy bear.

The voices of the angered elves echoed in his mind, along with the caramel-smooth croon of Cornelius Bandersnatch and his promises of a better life beyond the confines of the village, and the sad, defeated voice of Bushy Evergreen. Nothing was ever going to be the same again.

Loudest of all was the voice in his own head telling him that it was all his own fault.

There was nothing for it – he would have to speak with Santa.

Eighteen

THE OFFER OF A LIFETIME

'Santa?'

Alabaster rapped on the door to Santa's office.

'Just a moment,' a voice called from within. Then: 'Enter!'

Alabaster pushed open the door to find Cornelius at Santa's desk, its varnished surface covered in sheets of paper. Cornelius smiled up at him over the top of horn-rimmed spectacles, the tips of each of his bony fingers pressed to the matching digit of the other hand.

'Don't just stand there, do come in, dear boy.'

Alabaster obliged.

'How may I be of assistance?'

'Where's Santa?' Alabaster demanded.

Cornelius took off his glasses and thoughtfully sucked the tip, observing the new arrival.

'I'm afraid you won't find him here, Mister...?'

The question hung in the air, while Alabaster decided whether or not to complete his sentence. It seemed rude not to. 'Alabaster Snowball, sir.'

'Ah, Alabaster Snowball,' the slender man repeated, as though it had been on the tip of his tongue all along. 'I am charmed to finally make your acquaintance.' He extended his hand, which Alabaster found himself shaking, before it had even occurred to him whether he wanted to or not. 'Santa has told me so much about you; one of his most talented elves, as I recall.'

Alabaster blinked. 'Santa said that?'

'Absolutely. And from the man himself, I must say that is quite the compliment.'

Alabaster was taken aback. After all the ideas Santa had personally rejected... he believed his ideas were still valuable?

'Do take a seat, Alabaster. I want to know everything.'

'Everything, sir?'

'Your ambitions, Alabaster. Your dreams, your goals. Where do you see yourself in fifty years' time?'

'Well, sir,' he began, unable to shake the feeling of unease now rising within him. He had come to speak with Santa, not the stranger across from him, with that expectant look on his face. Nonetheless, it seemed inappropriate not to respond. 'I wish to be an inventor.'

'An inventor!' Cornelius clapped his hands with delight. 'How wonderful! But what is this talk of wishing, Alabaster? Do you awaken every morning with new ideas for inventions brimming inside your mind?'

'Yes, sir...'

'And do you spend sleepless nights, poring over new ideas, simply exhilarated by the endless possibilities, the wonders you could achieve, the prestige that is due to you for being so utterly and effortlessly brilliant, my dear boy?'

'Why, yes sir,' Alabaster agreed. There was no point lying. In fact, it was altogether quite remarkable how accurate Cornelius's assessment was; almost as if he already knew him inside and out.

'Then, let me tell you something. Alabaster, my boy; you *are* an inventor. In your heart and in your mind, and that's what truly matters. No man's destiny can be delayed indefinitely, no matter the obstacles.' He peered at the elf quizzically. 'So, tell me, Alabaster... for what earthly reason does your ambition remain unfulfilled?'

Alabaster shuffled nervously in his seat. 'I haven't been given the opportunity, sir.'

Cornelius looked taken aback. Mortified. 'Not been given the... my dear boy, this is an injustice of the highest degree, a travesty. To deny an elf his calling...

93

why, that is insufferable. Especially one as talented and brilliant as you.'

Alabaster could not help but feel as though he had been truly seen for the first time.

'To tell you the absolute truth, Alabaster, our meeting could not have come at a more opportune moment. You see, as it happens, my Chief Toy Inventor happens to be entering retirement this very weekend. I will be looking to appoint a replacement and, frankly, I would be honoured if you would consider putting your talents to work at my factory. It strikes me that you would fit the bill perfectly.'

Alabaster sat, open-mouthed. It was all he had ever wanted. All standing before him. Right there, on a plate.

'I need to talk to Santa…'

'But of course,' Cornelius said. 'The two of you have much to discuss, I'm certain. Between you and me, Alabaster, there really is no future here. Production has ceased indefinitely, almost certainly for ever. Even when it was in full swing, those who recognised your value and privately acknowledged how much you had to offer chose to stand in your way. Those wondrous, unique talents of yours, swirling down the drain. Stick with me, and everything you have ever worked for, everything you have ever dreamed of, will finally become fulfilled. Think of all the happiness you will be able to bring to those children who have, for too long, been denied your special gifts.'

Then he got out of his chair and patted Alabaster on the back. 'Think it over, won't you? We leave for London at noon tomorrow. I have organised transportation for all that wish to take advantage of the opportunity being offered here.'

As Cornelius led Alabaster to the door, he paused suddenly, stopping short of the doorknob. He leaned down to speak to the elf in a conspiratorial whisper.

'I do have one little question…'

'Yes, Mister Bandersnatch?'

He felt the hot glare of Cornelius's eyes on his body as they scanned up and down his broad-but-diminutive frame, the slightest hint of distate on his lips.

'Is that… *soot*… on your outfit?'

Alabaster gulped. He had never cleaned it off. Before he could answer, Cornelius continued:

'Do please ensure it is thoroughly cleaned before you decide to join us, there's a good chap. One undeniable advantage of working in the human world is that you will have no need of travelling by chimney anymore.'

He gave Alabaster a wink, and gently ushered the elf out the door before closing it behind him.

Nineteen

FINDING SANTA

Everything you ever dreamed of...

Cornelius's words spun around and around in Alabaster's head, at once both as appealing as they were appalling. A burning shame rose within him for allowing himself to think of it. Still, the echoes of Cornelius's voice persisted.

We leave tomorrow at noon.

That gave him less than twenty-four hours to come to a decision. Even entertaining the possibility of deserting Santa felt like he was breaking a promise. And yet, there it was, standing before him in glorious technicolor: Alabaster the inventor. Just think of it! The toys that would no longer exist only in his imagination, the scores upon scores of designs he would finally be allowed to bring to fruition, his fondest fantasies all breathed into life if he were simply to say the magic words to himself: yes, I will.

He had to speak to Santa. He could not leave without speaking to him. He couldn't begin to imagine how the old man might be feeling right now.

Alabaster searched the factory's rooms high and low, but Santa was nowhere to be found. The lifelessness of the usually-bustling, cheerful building was eerie and cold.

A voice pricked at his conscience: *You did this.*

Alabaster dreaded to think of what he would see the next time he unrolled the naughty list.

Perhaps he would find Santa at his private quarters. If not there, then he would try somewhere else – he would leave no cranny unexplored. He descended the stairs until he reached the lobby, where a handful of elves still remained, some engaged in deep conversation, others looking shell-shocked and forlorn. Among them, Mary stood alone, looking through the glass doors into the distance. Alabaster was relieved to see her.

'Mary, have you seen Santa anywhere?'

She shook her head. 'I haven't seen him since Cornelius arrived.'

She looked into his eyes, the corners of her mouth tight and sad.

'I don't know what to do,' she said. 'Everything has changed so suddenly. I'm frightened.'

The sight of Mary's welling tears made Alabaster turn his own gaze to the ground.

'Mary, I want you to know... I'm sorry. About everything.'

'The cake, you mean?'

Alabaster did not reply.

'We have a lot to think about right now. A birthday cake is the least of our worries. Promise me we'll stick together?'

Alabaster took her hand. 'Of course.'

❀ ❀ ❀

There was no sign of Santa at his private quarters either. Standing on Alabaster's shoulders, Mary wiped the ice-covered window with a sleeve and peered inside.

'There's not so much as a light on,' she called down to him.

'Can't you see anything at all?'

Alabaster felt a shift of weight on his shoulders, and lurched for balance as she peered through another section of window. 'Nothing out of the ordinary. It looks just as it always does.'

Grunting, Alabaster bent his knees and lowered Mary onto the ground.

'What now?'

'I've no idea.'

Suddenly, from the side of the building they heard a low rumbling and the clank of chains.

The stables!

They hurried around the corner to see the head of Dasher protruding from an open-topped door. In front of him was Santa, dressed in brown, softly stroking the animal's head.

'You won't be needing this, this year,' he was saying, as he removed the bridle. Dasher lowered his head and murmured softly, as though he understood. Santa patted the reindeer's back. 'We'll be all right boy, I'll look after you just as I always have.'

His free hand held a fistful of bridles that he had collected already from the other reindeer.

Mary and Alabaster exchanged a look. The Big Man was unaware of their presence. Mary let out a cough.

Santa turned his head and peered down at the elf. 'Alabaster?'

'Yes, sir.' For want of anything else to say, he offered meekly, 'How are you?'

Santa offered a mirthless smile. 'All things considered, my friends, I've had better days.'

There was so much that Alabaster had planned to say. Now that the opportunity had arrived, his mind was a complete blank. Should he admit the truth about what had happened, how he alone was responsible for Cornelius Bandersnatch finding the Grotto? What good would it do? It certainly wouldn't remedy the situation.

Finally, it was Mary who spoke up for both of them.

'Is there anything at all that we can do?'

The old man's face, now robbed of its jovial glow, bore the creases and marks of every one of his ageless years; the face of a man who had lived for all eternity and it had finally begun to show.

'I'm afraid what's done is done. There is no future here.'

'That's not tr-' Mary began, but was stopped by a wave of Santa's hand.

He let out a lengthy sigh. 'The most difficult thing to admit, even to myself, is that the situation we now find ourselves in is all of my own making.'

Alabaster desperately wanted to interject, to tell him that he was wrong. That it was the fault of a disobedient elf who possessed the arrogance to believe that he knew better than Santa Claus.

But he did not.

Santa continued: 'It was unwise of me to have believed that I alone could keep the spirit of Christmas alive all this time. The world beyond these frozen parts is a hard, cold place. Every year it seems to grows ever more so. While we go about our lives cocooned from the human world here in the safety of the Grotto, we remain ignorant of it, of how – like the seasons – everything is destined to change. Yes, I possess the magic to slow time to undertake my annual duties, but nobody can hold back the constant march of time.'

Alabaster could not believe what he was hearing. 'But Santa, you can't give up. The world's children depend on you.'

Santa looked at him sadly.

'Things are different now. People value different things. They mistrust what is good. My only intention truly was to bring joy to this world. When people are determined to find cause for hate, it is altogether too easy find it. They say I am a criminal, that the whole enterprise is to fulfil some selfish need in myself to be admired and adored, and that I am causing grave damage in the process. Who am I to tell them that they are wrong? Perhaps *I* ought to admit they are right.'

Alabaster could never in his wildest dreams have imagined any event that could bring Santa, of all people, to such a state of hopelessness.

'Take my advice,' he said solemnly. 'Go with Cornelius. He is able to offer you more than I can. All I can hope is that, when the inevitable comes, I can find somewhere to put down roots, and look after those that truly depend on me.' He reached into the stable as he gave Dasher a broad stroke of his bare hand. 'I owe them that.'

Twenty

THE FINAL STRAW

Alabaster and Mary walked home. The shock of it all was a heavy burden to bear. Mary commented that she had never seen Santa so awfully sad in all of her hundred-or-so years; Alabaster felt too terrible to offer any comment. Anything he could say would make him feel an even bigger fraud.

At Alabaster's house, he had just inserted his key in the lock when an earth-shattering noise came from within. If he wasn't much mistaken, it was the sound of a tree crashing to the ground.

Alabaster winced.

'What was that?' Mary asked.

'On second thoughts,' Alabaster said quickly,

'shouldn't it be me that offers you the walk home? It's the gentlemanly thing to do, after all.'

He offered his arm with a smile. He would have to deal with the carnage later.

'If you insist,' Mary said, and tucked her arm inside the crook of his elbow.

✿ ✿ ✿

The walk to Mary's home was only five minutes from Alabaster's, and the evening was fresh and clear. Every house they passed was busy with activity; neighbouring inhabitants pulled down Christmas decorations, folded up belongings intended for keeping, and put out others that were to be discarded. Families within called up and down stairs while they frantically packed.

'I suppose I had better make a start too,' Mary said, when they arrived at her door. 'I hardly know where to begin; it all seems so surreal.'

Alabaster nodded.

'Can I invite you in for a tea?' she asked.

The last thing Alabaster wanted right now was to be alone. But he shook his head solemnly.

'I wish I could,' he said. 'I have a lot that needs to be taken care of before tomorrow.'

'Good night, then,' she said. 'I'll wait for you in the morning.'

'I'll be here at nine o'clock sharp,' Alabaster promised. 'Good night, Mary.'

❊ ❊ ❊

The sight that awaited Alabaster upon his return was as devastating as was to be expected: the Christmas tree had been razed to the floor, its remains strewn across every inch of carpet. The sharp splinters of baubles, fractured and smashed to smithereens, glinted from every corner. A faint electrical buzz hummed and fizzed as a string of fairy lights flickered lifelessly before petering out. Overturned chairs and tables and a severed, splintered leg bore evidence of the war that had preceded Alabaster's arrival, and had probably gone on all afternoon. In the midst of the chaos sat the krampus, a string of tinsel clamped in its jaws, its tail wagging frantically to see its owner.

Alabaster was in no mood for it. Because of you, he thought angrily, the house is a mess. Because of you, I can't bring Mary into my own home. Because of you, the Grotto is no longer in operation. As painful as it was to admit, there were no other conclusions to be drawn: things would have been better had the krampus never entered his life.

Without saying a word, Alabaster retrieved his haversack from the upturned coat-stand. The krampus leapt around the mess playfully, blissfully unaware that he had done anything to upset its owner.

Alabaster lay the bag open on the floor beside the excited cub. Realising it was now too large to fit inside his haversack, he emptied out a burlap sack that had been filled with potatoes, and scooped up the animal inside.

'I'm sorry, Fluffy,' he said, 'but it's time for you go.'

Twenty-One

THIRD TIME'S A CHARM

The journey to the foot of Mount Halti was more difficult than ever. Fluffy was now several times as large as it had been on their first encounter and, after a half a mile or so of being carried in the sack, felt easily ten times heavier than that.

The evening was crisp and wisps of a breeze sliced at Alabaster's reddened cheeks as he trundled along the path to the foot of the mountain.

He stopped and heaved the contents of the sack onto the snow-covered ground with a grunt. The cub leapt out and trotted about, imprinting the snow with the goat-prints of its hind legs, its long, pointed tongue hanging from the corner of its mouth like an excited puppy.

Alabaster knelt beside the animal and gave its coarse fur a gentle stroke, all the while taking deep breaths so as not to allow himself to cry.

In turn, Fluffy rubbed against Alabaster with horns that, now long and sharp, had begun to curl back on themselves like those of a ram. The little creature's long, tufted tail flicked back and forth, brushing snake-like trails in the snow.

'I'm sorry, my friend,' Alabaster said. 'This is where we say good-'

Suddenly, the creature lunged forward and snapped at the finger of Alabaster's glove. Pulling back and wriggling its head, it snatched the glove clean off and darted away.

'Hey, come back with that!'

Alabaster chased after the animal, who paused to look back at him, then ran further on.

'Fluffy, wait!'

Alabaster continued to run, falling into the snow. The cub abruptly stopped.

'Bad Fluffy!' he chided. Then he saw what the animal was looking at.

Before them, in the middle of the snow, lay a great swirling mass of grey. An enormous whirlpool, but one made of electrified mud and ice. Trails of long white snow-threads circled inwards towards the epicentre, which gaped open like a big black hole. Its edges glowed, emitting an occasional electric fizzle, miniature bolts of lightning crackling from one end to the other.

'What on earth…?' Alabaster's words trailed off into nothingness, as though swallowed into the swirling pit.

The krampus turned its head towards Alabaster and fixed him with a peculiar gaze that suddenly seemed wise, knowing… and excited. If it had only had language, Alabaster felt sure that he could have told him exactly what they were looking at.

Frightened, Alabaster got to his feet and took a step backwards. 'Hey, come back from there,' he warned, beckoning the animal with his hand. It did not respond, so he grabbed one of its horns and attempted to pull it to safety.

The creature let out an ear-splitting honk and butted Alabaster hard in the stomach, knocking him to the ground. It snorted loudly, scuffing its front claws in the snow, plumes of white mist blowing from its nostrils. Then, with its back to Alabaster, it returned its gaze to the void. After giving its bottom a little wriggle, to Alabaster's horror, the creature leapt headfirst into the eye of the strange whirlpool.

'Fluffy, no!'

For a moment, the animal's silhouette remained imprinted across the surface of the whirlpool's mouth, an electric blue cloud that lingered in the air.

'Fluffy?' Alabaster gasped. 'Fluffy!'

In desperation, he grabbed the sack and dropped it into the pool. The bottom felt like icy water. He drew sackfuls, the neon liquid gushing through the woven holes in the bottom making it glow pink, as if its own magic were somehow becoming woven into the very fabric of the sack.

After filling several dozen sackfuls, Alabaster had to admit defeat.

Fluffy was gone.

Twenty-Two

PACKING TO DO

Closing the door behind him, Alabaster kicked off his snowshoes and crumpled into a ball.

This wasn't how he had imagined it ending.

Was Fluffy… dead?

He sobbed quietly, suddenly feeling very alone. The house, though still in a state of distress, was deathly silent. A long night of cleaning and packing still lay ahead of him, but he could barely bring himself to move.

Worst of all was not knowing what had become of the little creature, the only thing he could call a friend.

'Alabaster Snowball,' he muttered to himself. 'You are one selfish elf.'

He pulled himself to his feet and looked about at the debris, wiping away the blur of tears that clouded his vision.

As much of a mess as the krampus had made, the explosion of Christmas debris that now lay before him was the last shred of evidence that it had ever existed. Besides, the fallen tree, the broken table, the upturned chair and all the rest of it didn't begin to compare to the chaos that Alabaster himself had set in motion.

There was so much to do. He urged himself to snap out of it. To look at it as a fresh beginning, a new chapter. He couldn't change what had happened, but he did have the chance to start anew. There was comfort to be found in that.

And so, he set about the arduous task of clearing the debris. After sweeping up the fallen tree's pine needles from the carpet, he bundled its remains into a bag and placed it outside the door. He filled his suitcase with the clothes that he would need for his new home, and set aside those that he would need for tomorrow's journey. No matter how he tried, the tell-tale traces of soot would not budge from his work tunic. He collected an assortment of notebooks and parchments containing sketches and blueprints for his inventions, placed them on top of his folded clothes and closed the suitcase lid.

After resetting the table in the corner of the room, he placed the broken leg in its usual position to stop it from toppling, when he noticed something that had fallen behind.

The mahogony box. The naughty list!

Careful not to knock the balanced leg, Alabaster retrieved the box and carried it to the sofa, avoiding the shards of broken bauble. He sat and gazed at the closed box for a minute, almost scared to look inside.

Finally, he unrolled the parchment. Among the names listed among the 'S's, there was his:

Name: Alabaster Snowball (94);
Region: Lapland;
Misdemeanour: Venturing beyond the Elfland boundary – TWICE;
Defying Santa's instructions and taking in the krampus cub as a pet;
Breaking and entering Santa's workshop – TWICE;
Stealing the Infinity Crystal;
Using the invisibility charm to eavesdrop on Santa's private conversations.

Alabaster cringed to read every new entry, their fresh lettering shining that little more brightly in golden ink beside his name.

'I'm a criminal,' he said. His heart sank like lead into his boots.

With a groan, he wrapped up the scroll, placed it

back in its box and put it on top of the other items in his suitcase.

He turned out the bedside lamp and fell into a restless, slumber, haunted by the sight of the krampus disappearing into the mysterious void.

Twenty-Three

SON OF AN OGRE

The following morning, the village square bustled with movement and excitement. Throngs of elves stood dressed in their winter coats, with suitcases and bags in hand. An air of anxious chattering hung over them as they waited – for what they did not quite know. A light peppering of snow lingered in the air, a sunless, twilight glow emanating from beyond the crown of treetops to the east.

'Look how many there are,' Alabaster exclaimed in astonishment. 'How does Cornelius intend to carry us all to London?'

Mary looked skeptical. 'He didn't say how exactly; he just said that transportation had been arranged.'

Alabaster looked at his watch. Eleven fifty-five.

'What's that noise?'

From the distance, there came a soft humming sound, barely perceptible at first, but one that steadily grew as, one by one, each of the elves turned to see where the din was coming from.

Then it came.

Appearing over the horizon like an enormous white cigar, Cornelius's promised means of transportation had arrived. A great airship, emblazoned with the words 'Bandersnatch Toys' and an image of Cornelius's beaming face, hovered towards them. As it approached, the propellors buzzed ever louder, evolving into an incessant *chop-chop-chop*... The congregated crowd cooed in amazement.

'Have you ever seen such a thing?'

'Well, I never...'

'Behold, elves, elvettes and elflings!' The voice of Cornelius Bandersnatch rang out over a megaphone. 'The Bandsdersnatch Airbus has arrived!'

The airship glided closer and closer, until its furrowed belly hovered directly above them. The propellers' axes tilted and the ship slowly began its descent.

Attached to the underside of the balloon was a large metal compartment the size of several double-decker buses. Here is where Cornelius stood, barking through his megaphone out of an open glass window.

'Roll up, roll up, all that intend to embark on our exciting new adventure!'

When the ship finally came to a stop, Cornelius flung open the door and gestured for the elves to enter.

'Please take your seats, ladies and gentlemen. The adventure of a lifetime beckons – your carriage awaits!'

The elves cheered in unison. As they boarded, Cornelius ushered the eager elves to their rows of seats. Mary and Alabaster exchanged a dark look.

'You're not actually going through with this, are you, Mary?'

They turned to see Bushy Evergreen.

'Uncle!' Mary threw her arms around the old elf, taking him quite by surprise. 'I'm so glad to see you!'

'So this is how it all ends, hm? Carried away in an overblown hot air balloon.' He chuckled drily. 'I would have expected nothing less from one such as him; full of nothing but hot air!'

Mary looked guiltily at the ground. 'Uncle, I'm so sorry…'

'Stay with me, Mary.' The frailty of the old elf suddenly shone through. Despite his crotchety demeanour, there was no denying the vulnerability of one so old. Mary bit her lip, visibly torn.

'Why don't you come with us?' Alabaster said.

'You?!' Bushy's face turned into a hateful sneer. 'You've changed your tune! What happened to all that stuff you were saying only yesterday? Don't tell me. Offered you a position, hasn't he? Told you to come and be inventor-in-chief at his factory. The trouble with you, Alabaster – you think your heart is in the right place, but where is your integrity? That's the trouble with letting yourself be driven by your ambition – it leaves you open to manipulation. A bunch of empty promises, and you're anybody's!'

Bushy did not look so vulnerable now. A furnace of unveiled contempt burned in Alabaster's direction.

'When Santa found you abandoned in the forests of Oslo all those years ago, I told him nothing good would come of it,' Bushy hissed. 'You are a *Wild Elf*. Wild Elves are not to be trusted. Mary, I forbid you to go with him. You were brought up to be better than that.'

Mary looked at her uncle in horror. Tears of anger welled in her eyes.

'No, uncle,' she said, her voice wavering. 'Alabaster is my friend...'

'And I am your family.' Bushy took Mary's hand and held it so tightly that the freckles on his paper-thin knuckles turned white. 'Blood is thicker than... whatever slime runs through the veins of a no-good son-of-an-ogre like this one.'

Suddenly, it all became clear. All the ideas that Alabaster had presented to the senior panel had been shot down in flames because of where he had come from, not who he was. More than anything, Alabaster wished he had never done a wrong thing in his life. At least then he could show the old elf that being a Wild Elf did not mean he was a wicked elf. And yet, there was the list of misdemeanours beside his name on the naughty list. It was too late to change it, though he would have given anything to do so. All he could do now was start again, with someone who *would* give him a chance.

'I'm going,' Alabaster said. 'Wild Elf or not, I deserve a chance like anyone else. And Mary is coming with me. I'm not leaving without you, Mary.'

Cornelius's voice rang out:

'Final call for any and all elves.' Apart from a final handful queued at the airship's door, the entire throng had managed to make their way aboard.

'Uncle, let me go!' Mary pleaded.

'Your mother would roll in her grave if she could see this. Her own daughter, abandoning her own family, abandoning Santa! I won't have it!'

'I said, let me go!' Mary wrestled her arm from Bushy's grip, and the old elf fell to the ground, letting out a cry as he landed hard on the frosty tarmac. Alabaster reached forward to help him up.

'Don't you touch me!' he hissed, swiping at him with his walking stick. 'I hope you'll be happy, the two of you. I had you figured out all along, but *you*, Mary. I don't know you at all. Go and enjoy your lives together. You deserve each other.'

Mary and Alabaster picked up their luggage and turned to run towards the airship.

But it was too late. The airship, now twenty feet in the air and rising, had already made its departure.

Twenty-Four

A WILD SOLUTION

Mary and Alabaster watched in horror as the blimp rose higher. The propellers tilted again on their axes and the ship began to sail due south. All was lost. Cornelius's promise of finally fulfilling Alabaster's dream; the new life he had planned to build with Mary in London – all dashed. They were stuck there forever.

Unless…

Suddenly, Alabaster had an idea.

He offered Mary his hand. 'Come with me!'

Mary hesitated. 'But… our things!'

'Don't worry,' he said. He snatched her by the fingertips and led her along the path, back the way they had come. 'We'll be back in a jiffy!'

At a pace, he led Mary through the deserted streets, past the workshop, past the enormous Christmas tree until, finally, they reached the garden of Alabaster's house.

'Wait here,' he instructed. Mary obliged, watching as he rummaged through the collection of discarded items leaning against the outside wall. 'A-ha!' Finally, he emerged, holding aloft a large flat piece of wood. Beaming a victorious smile, he sprinted back to Mary with the board tucked under his arm.

He laid it flat on the floor, the smooth, curved underside pointing upwards, and took a pouch from his belt. He sprinkled a pinch of its contents along the wooden surface, before rubbing it in with the open palm of his hand.

'What is that?'

'Questions later.' Alabaster turned over the board and climbed aboard. He seized hold of the rope attached to the front. 'It's going to be a tight squeeze, but I think it should just about hold the both of us.'

Mary looked unconvinced, but took her place behind him on the board.

'Whatever you do, just keep hold of me,' he said, securing her arms around the trunk of his body. 'You got me?'

'I think so,' came Mary's voice in his ear, her warm breath casting a pleasant tingle against the nape of his neck.

'Then here we go!' Alabaster cried. His foot kicked in the snow, setting the board in motion so that it careened gently down the icy path. In the distance, the airship appeared no bigger than a speck, seeming hardly to move at all. He tugged at the rope and the board rose steadily upward.

Mary let out a gasp, her grip tightening around him. 'We… we're flying!'

'Yep!' Alabaster let out a laugh. 'Are you ok back there?'

After a pause, her voice came in his ear, shaky and uncertain. 'I guess so. I've never flown before.'

'Just hold on.'

As they glided towards the village square, he relaxed his grip on the rope and the board made a gentle descent until they were once again coasting along on solid snow.

'Be ready,' Alabaster warned, as their suitcases approached. 'Three… two… NOW!'

The snurfer's pace slowed a little as Alabaster manoeuvred between their standing suitcases, each managing to grab the handle of their own as they passed. Mary's arm, now carrying her luggage, whipped around Alabaster's chest, almost knocking him off-balance.

'Careful!' he cried. He tugged on the rope, and the snurfer rose once again until it was hovering above the ground. Without the friction of snow to slow it down, it continued to gather speed. Not quite as swiftly as before; Alabaster supposed it was the extra weight of their suitcases. Nonetheless, the blimp in the distance seemed to grow ever so slightly larger as they approached.

'We're going to make it!' Alabaster cheered as the whirling propellers came into clear view.

Hazy, ice-cold threads of mist burned at their faces as the snurfer continued its climb, growing steadily into a dense white fog that obscured their vision. Soon, they found themselves flying blind, coasting through a thick plume of cloud.

'Alabaster, I can't see!' Mary shrieked, palpable terror in her voice.

'We're almost there, hold on!'

Hurtling at such great speed, anything could appear through the clouds and collide with them at any moment.

'My hands are so cold,' she cried, 'I don't think I can.'

Alabaster pressed his hand to hers, tautening the rope and causing them to rise ever higher.

Finally they pierced the crown of dense haze, and it seemed they were floating high above a carpet of candyfloss. The pink twilight of a hidden sun burst over the horizon, its rays painting the sky and everything below with such beauty that Alabaster could do little more than gasp in awe.

The *chop-chop-chop* of the airship's propellers

sounded very loud now. Alabaster looked up to see that they were now coasting directly beneath it, by a matter of feet.

Their only hope was to navigate themselves in line with the undercarriage and pray someone would be able to open the compartment door.

Steering the snurfer gently leftward, Alabaster managed to haul themselves up in line with the glass windows of the gondola. Inside, hundreds of elves sat in rows, gazing upon the spectacular panorama with delight and awe. One infant elf, upon seeing Alabaster and Mary aboard the flying contraption, rubbed his eyes with disbelief.

'Help us!' Alabaster called, the words trailing yards behind the moment they left his mouth. 'Please!'

The little elf tugged at his mother's sleeve and pointed. With bulging eyes, she rose from her seat and gesticulated wildly, raising her voice throughout the carriage. Cornelius, who had been sitting at the front of the compartment, rose and staggered towards the window. The carriage door slid open and he crouched at the doorway, gesturing for Alabaster to bring the board closer.

It was a task easier said than done; for some reason – turbulence, he supposed – the board was inclined to sway into the side of the compartment like a magnet. The second time it happened, Mary's suitcase fell from her grip and it tumbled into the clouds, never to be seen again.

Finally, Alabaster managed to align himself with the door.

'Pass me your case!'

Cornelius's words came silent amid the deafening wind, but Alabaster understood from his wild gestures what he was asking him to do. There was no way he could control the snurfer and pass Cornelius the suitcase at the same time. He tapped Mary's hand and passed the handle of his suitcase into her trembling, ice-cold fingers.

'You have to pass it, Mary,' he called at the top of his voice. 'You can do it!'

Clinging to Alabaster's chest for dear life, and trembling like a bowl of blancmange, Mary very slowly lifted the case. It was much heavier than hers had been, and it took all of her strength to support its weight as she extended her arm towards Cornelius's open hands.

A little closer, a little closer…

There!

As soon as Cornelius had relieved her of the load, Mary was caught off-balance and the board wobbled dangerously beneath her feet. In panic, she threw her free arm around Alabaster's shoulder.

'Give me your hand!' Cornelius's mouth was saying, his own hand outstretched.

Beneath their feet, the clouds were thinning. A vast expanse of water lay below, with oddly-shaped clusters of land marked with roads and pathways, filled with rows upon rows of tiny buildings and cars. It was a sheer drop of certain death were she to make one false move.

'Don't look down!'

Closing her eyes, Mary held out her arm to take Cornelius's hand.

Taking one last big breath, she leapt, throwing herself towards him with all of her might.

Twenty-Five

ALL ABOARD

As Mary sprang from the board, the snurfer gave a sharp backward lurch beneath Alabaster's feet. While doing everything in his power to maintain his balance, the board veered sideways, knocking him and it into the side of the carriage. He yanked hard at the rope, blistering his reddened palms. He had to stay aboard, no matter what. And somehow regain control. Slowly but surely, the carriage was slipping ahead of him, the faces of the passengers pressed to the window.

Behind him, the incessant *chop-chop-chop* of the propellers – louder than thunder now – advanced toward him, like the jaws of a predatory animal snapping at his heels.

It was then that Alabaster noted the fatal flaw in the snurfer's design: with a pull of the rope he could steer the board left and right and, with a shift of his body weight, make it rise higher or lower, but there was no way to make the board gain forward momentum.

His only hope for survival now was to try and navigate the board away from the airship. He pulled at the rope, but it would not budge. Again he tried, pulling with all of his might, but nothing he did made any difference. Then he realised: he was being pulled directly into the spinning blades of the propeller.

There was no way out now. He pressed his hand to the glass windows, desperately trying to stop the backward pull with the tips of his fingers, but could not gain purchase on any of the smooth grooves that separated them. He banged on the windows in a final attempt to save himself.

'Help me!' he screamed.

Chop-chop-chop-chop-chop...

Alabaster closed his eyes, and prepared for certain doom.

Suddenly, he felt an arm reach across his chest and, with a hard yank, pull him through an open window. The momentum sent him sprawling into the air before landing on his back with a hard bump. A painful burning sensation tore across his palms as the rope wrenched itself from his grasp, followed by a loud crunching noise as the snurfer was eaten to splinters by the airship's hungry propellers. The airship gave a violent shake, and the elves let out a shriek of alarm, gripping onto whatever was available to regain their balance.

Alabaster, now supine on the floor, opened his eyes. A sea of faces peered down at him, blinking and concerned.

Then one of them said, 'Alabaster Snowball, you absolute idiot!'

It was Needles.

'What on earth do you think you were doing out there? It was a good job I managed to get that window open.'

Alabaster groaned as he pulled himself up onto his bottom and rubbed his head with sore and bleeding palms. It took a moment for his vision to correct itself, for the spots behind his eyes to vanish and for the double-of-everything to settle into one. Still his head pounded, and his hands burned raw with the cold. He hissed as the pain finally hit him.

'A thank you wouldn't go amiss,' Needles was going on. 'After all, I did save your life. Big oaf.'

'Give him room,' a voice admonished.

'Where's Mary?' Alabaster said, trying to move life into his frozen fingers. 'Is she safe?'

'I'm here,' Mary said. Her hair was a wild mess, her face still blanched from the shock of their ordeal.

Alabaster got to his feet and gave her a hug. Mary had lost her suitcase, and Alabaster the snurfer, but only one thing really mattered: they had survived to tell the tale.

'Promise me one thing,' Mary said, her hold on him loosening. Alabaster refused to let go.

'What's that?' he asked, the bottom of his chin resting in the crook of her shoulder.

'You never, ever ask me to do that again.'

'I won't, Mary.'

Finally relaxed, Mary's head rested against his.

Part Two

LONDON

Twenty-Six

LONDON

'Alabaster…' Mary whispered, shaking him awake. 'Alabaster, we're here!'

'Hm?' Alabaster opened one eye. Remembering where he was, he sat bolt upright and looked out the window.

Through a sheet of rain, an illuminated skyline of towers, cranes, and bridges sparkled against a bruised charcoal sky. The near-distant roar of traffic, hissing buses and beeping horns below indicated that they were in a place that was always in a hurry.

'Welcome to London, my dear elf friends,' Cornelius crooned through the intercom speaker as the airship hovered above a large flat roof of one of the buildings. 'Thank you for flying Bandersnatch Airways.' At this, he let out a chuckle. 'We shall be disembarking shortly; please ensure you take all of your belongings with you.'

Murmuring with excitement, the passengers rose to their feet and retrieved their luggage from beneath their seats. Meanwhile, Cornelius's gangly figure rose at the front of the carriage and yanked down the window of the door compartment. His eyes lit up, having seen something that clearly pleased him.

'Ah, my assistants,' he smiled.

Alabaster peered through the rain-spattered window to see a broad silhouette on the rooftop below. He let out a gasp. It was a Wild Elf, just like him. The figure's thick, hairy hands took hold of a rope tethered to the front of the undercarriage and wound it inwards, towards what Alabaster supposed was the ship's port. As they dipped ever closer, another figure came into view. She was standing beneath the canopy, a cascade of fiery red hair pouring from her crown. She held a knotted wooden staff in her hands, the head of which glowed a bright, emerald green.

'Ladies and gentlemen, it gives me great pleasure to introduce to you my loyal assistants, Kobold and Nixie,' Cornelius announced, as the ship completed its descent. 'I have no doubt they will make you feel extremely welcome in your new home.'

A deafening silence fell over the carriage. Under their breath, someone commented in astonishment, 'Wild Elves!'

'Indeed, they are,' Cornelius said in a matter-of-fact manner, 'and I'm afraid there's not much to be done about that. But rest assured, being elf-folk themselves, they are your brethren – we are all one big happy family here.'

His face wore the smile of a crocodile.

Cornelius flung open the carriage door and the elves filed out onto the wet roof, before uniformly scurrying beneath the shelter of the tarpaulin awning where Kobold and Nixie waited to greet them. As the last of the elves joined the huddled mass, the face of one of the Wild Elves – Kobold, Alabaster supposed – broke into a secretive smirk that made him shudder.

An enormous toy rocket, several metres tall, stood at a tilted angle at the edge of the roof. Its red and white stripes were illuminated by the flickering strobe of more than a hundred yellow light bulbs that spelled out the legend: 'Bandersnatch Toys Ltd', matching the logo emblazoned across the airship.

'Quickly,' Cornelius declared, 'let us get out of the rain so we may show you to your quarters.' He spun around swiftly and pushed open a pair of black metal doors. 'I'm sure that after such a long journey, everyone will want to retire for the evening.'

'Are you kidding?' a voice called out. 'We want to

explore!'

Cornelius chuckled. 'Now, now. There will be more than enough time for that. Tonight, you shall make yourselves comfortable in your sleeping quarters. The morning alarm will sound at six prompt, after which there will be breakfast until six-thirty, and then my assistants and I will show you around the workshop.'

He led the elves into the bowels of the building, down a long, metal staircase. After they had descended three or four flights, an entranceway appeared, a rectangular hole in the wall that led into the shadows of an unlit corridor.

Cornelius turned to peer amongst the crowd.

'Where is Mister Snowball?'

Alabaster took his hand from Mary's and held it up.

'I will show you to your quarters.'

Alabaster's heart sank. 'But, Mary…'

Cornelius chuckled and rolled his eyes. 'Fear not, noble Alabaster,' he said, reaching over the heads of the elves for Alabaster's hand. 'Mary will be escorted to her own quarters with the others.'

Mary offered an encouraging smile. 'It's ok. Really. I will see you in the morning.'

Alabaster frowned. An uneasy feeling welled up inside him. He had promised himself he would not let Mary go. And yet…

'The chamber for the chief inventor is on this floor,'

Cornelius said.

With a swish of his cape, he swept away into the hole, leading the way. Alabaster picked up his suitcase and, leaving Mary a final apologetic glance, followed him into the corridor.

❀ ❀ ❀

'I do hope you like your room,' Cornelius said, his bony fingers working to unfasten the last of several thick metal bolts fixed to the door's exterior. Alabaster hoped so too. All he had seen of the building so far had been black and cold; thousands of miles from home and no way to get back.

'It's not much,' Cornelius said, twisting the handle, 'but it's yours to call home.'

Alabaster stepped inside. He set down his suitcase and gawped at his new surroundings.

In stark contrast with the dark, damp stairwell from which they had just arrived, the room – and its homely aroma of dry wood chippings and candle wax – was clean and inviting. A ladder climbed to an elevated bed which overlooked the studio, a children's slide leading away from it at the other. A writing desk and a work bench were tucked neatly beneath. At the far end, a column of pine shelving designed around a spiral staircase contained all manner of fabrics, stencils, glues, paints and glitter; everything a toy inventor could wish for.

And it all belonged to him!

The rising euphoria was short-lived, however, and he offered Cornelius a weak smile.

'What's the matter?' Cornelius asked. 'Don't you like it?'

'I love it. I just wish Mary could see it too.'

Cornelius gave him a pat on the shoulder. 'Welcome to your playground, Alabaster. Everything you could possibly want is right here.'

Accepting Cornelius's words as an invitation to explore, Alabaster stepped forward and climbed the staircase. He did not know where to look first. He examined the labels of the closest boxes: pogo springs; rocket powder; rubber stops; axels and rods; washers, bolts, nails and screws.

He had found paradise on earth.

'Oh, thank you, Cornelius,' he said. 'Thank you, thank you! I'm sure I'll never want to leave.'

❋ ❋ ❋

'This way!' Kobold called, as he led the procession of elves down the winding staircase. Mary, following in step with the others, tried desperately not to cringe in fear as the shadows from his fiery torch darted and danced across the black painted walls.

Reaching the final step, Kobold nimbly hopped onto the stone floor and turned to address the crowd. They waited for him to speak in expectant silence.

Finally, indicating one of the corridors that tunnelled into the wall, he barked, 'Ladies, in the west wing. Gentlemen, in the east wing.'

Everybody stood unflinching for a moment. A murmur of dissatisfaction rippled through the crowd.

'Wait a moment,' a voice piped up. It was Needles. 'You don't intend to separate us?'

'Ladies, in the west wing,' Kobold repeated, his voice robotic, emotionless. 'Gentlemen, in the east wing.'

'You heard the elf,' Nixie barked, with an impatient clap of the hands. 'Let's get moving.'

Some of the elves jostled obediently towards the tunnel, when Alvin's voice rang out again.

'I'm not leaving my mum and my sisters,' Needles said, his arms folded across his chest. 'And if you think I will even entertain the idea, you're frankly out of your minds.'

Everybody froze. Dripping water against stone was the only sound that echoed in the darkness.

Kobold turned slowly to face him.

'I beg your pardon?' he said, his eyes narrowed.

Needles took a breath and puffed out his chest. 'We... we've been travelling for days. If we are to stay here as your guests, I demand that you do as we say.'

'Hear, hear,' agreed a handful of voices.

Kobold rolled his eyes impatiently. 'Nixie,' he said, his droll voice exuding boredom. 'Would you please see to our guest?'

'It would be my pleasure.' A wild grin cut across her face as she tucked her staff beneath her arm.

Needles, looking rather pleased with himself, stood with his head high, awaiting his reward.

Suddenly, a blinding flash of blue light shot from the end of Nixie's staff, accompanied by a loud electrical whip-crack.

When the elves opened their eyes, Needles was gone. All that was left of him was a pair of shoes, coated with fine grey dust.

Mary's hands flew to her mouth in horror. Still dazzled by the light, she could not quite believe her eyes.

Kobold gave the crowd a satisfied smirk. 'Does anybody else have similar demands?'

His question was met with dead silence.

'Very good,' he said. Then, with a flick of the thumb, he indicated the tunnel once more. 'Ladies in the west wing; gentlemen in the east wing. Let's go!'

Without argument, the elves filed into the corridor and separated into their designated chambers.

Twenty-Seven

THE TOY SHOP

Alabaster was awakened by a loud, insistent rapping at the door. He reached out for a bedside lamp that wasn't there, before finally remembering where he was.

Rat-tat-tat-tat-tat!

'Coming,' he called, and tossed his blanket aside. He could only wonder at the hour of the night – he had been so fired up with creative inspiration before going to bed that he had fallen into a deep sleep without remembering to unpack his alarm clock. He let himself down the slide and slipped smoothly along the varnished floor in his pyjamas. The door to his chamber did not have a peep-hole, so Alabaster turned the handle – which did not have an inside lock – and opened the door a crack to see who his visitor was.

It was Kobold and Nixie.

'Cornelius has requested the pleasure of your company,' they intoned together.

'What time is it?'

'It's six-thirty,' Kobold answered sharply. 'You've already missed breakfast.'

'Get dressed,' Nixie said, then gave an impatient clap of her hands. 'Quickly now, chop-chop!'

Alabaster obeyed, and soon they were once again winding their way down the steps of the pitch-black stairwell.

✿ ✿ ✿

Cornelius's toy shop, as Alabaster had correctly predicted, was a festive feast for the eyes. From the oversized baubles and bells that loomed overhead, to the human-sized animatronic tin soldiers and jack-in-the-boxes that burst forth on oversized springs, the shop seemed to have been designed to provide a snail's eye view of the world's most elaborate (not to mention ostentatious) Christmas tree. A toy train chugged its way around the spiralling walkway, leading in and out of different brightly lit, toy-themed caverns.

Cornelius, in the middle of the lobby, held his cane aloft as Alabaster approached.

'You've just missed the others,' he said, by way of a

greeting. 'What a shame! I had so wanted to give you all the grand tour at the same time, but it seems as though one particular elf – who shall remain nameless – forgot to set their alarm clock. Silly sausage.'

He shot Alabaster a strange smile. Had he not known Cornelius better, Alabaster might have suspected he was being mocked.

'Welcome to Cornelius's Caverns,' he said, 'the most magical place in the world!'

Alabaster could well believe him. The sheer volume and range of toys and games packed within a single blink was staggering. It almost put the Grotto to shame.

Almost.

Despite the opulent extravagance of his surroundings, Alabaster knew that nothing could truly compare to the magic of the real thing.

Cornelius was no Santa Claus.

'Come, let me give you a tour,' Cornelius said, leading the way. He proceeded along the shop floor with long strides that made the little elf break into a jog to keep up. He stopped at the first cavern, which contained a lavish display of plush animal toys of all shapes and sizes, and took a medium-sized teddy bear in his hands. He looked at it wistfully, before winding a little white string that protruded from its bottom around the length of his bony finger.

'Perhaps it is just as well that the others aren't here to join us,' he said, in a low voice. 'There are things that I am now permitted to divulge that I would never share with just anybody.'

He released the cord, and in a high-pitched monotone, the teddy bear's pre-recorded voice said, 'I want to be your friend!'

The whites of Cornelius's eyes flashed with delight. 'I trust that you feel the same.'

Once again, he tugged at the string and, again, the teddy spoke: 'I want to share all my secrets!'

A dark smile spread across Cornelius's face. 'I want to know everything.'

'How is Mary doing?' Alabaster asked. 'I wanted to see her.'

Cornelius's jaw appeared to tighten as he placed the teddy bear back on the shelf.

'Mary is delighted to be here,' he said, his sing-song voice rising and falling theatrically. 'And every bit as excited as I am to hear all about the ideas and plans of my new Senior Toy Inventor. Especially the secret behind the wondrous contraption that brought you to my airbus. What was it called...?'

'The snurfer.'

'The snurfer, yes.' His tongue flicked out and licked at the corner of his lipless mouth. 'Is there a child alive who wouldn't dream of taking flight aboard Alabaster

Snowball's Sensational Soaring Snurfer?'

Alabaster returned Cornelius's grin with an awkward half-smile.

'Mr Bandersnatch, sir – given what happened the other day, don't you think it could be a little – well – dangerous in the wrong hands?'

Cornelius chuckled. 'I've no doubt they would make an absolute killing, my boy.' He patted Alabaster on the back.

'In the hands of children, I mean.'

'Oh, poppycock – they're going to love it!'

Alabaster began to protest, but Cornelius barely allowed him time to catch a breath.

'I don't know how you did it – some sort of in-built drone technology, I shouldn't wonder? Or a sprinkling of that infamous Wild Elf magic? It doesn't altogether matter how you did it, I love it. In fact, I love it so much, we are planning to mount its official launch on Christmas Day, in this very toy shop.'

'Official launch…?'

Cornelius, seemingly detecting a note of reticence, continued in a low, conspiratorial hush, 'We have a once-in-a-season smash hit on our hands, Alabaster; a Christmas best-seller that will make the pogo-stick look like a bargain-basement candy cane.'

Then he stopped and looked Alabaster in the eye.

'The big day is only a week away. If we are to

launch in time, we had better get going. All we need is the prototype and patent drawings, and we can begin manufacturing right away. You do have the patent drawings?'

Alabaster looked at him blankly.

'The designs for your invention?'

'Oh, no, it was something I invented as I went along…'

Cornelius furrowed his brow in concern. 'How long will it take to get them done?'

'An hour, perhaps,' Alabaster said, 'but…'

Cornelius straightened up.

'Then what are we waiting for? You must begin at once. Kobold! Nixie! Would you please escort our esteemed guest back to his workshop? He has magic to make.'

Kobold and Nixie reappeared, flanking Alabaster like prison guards.

Cornelius fixed him with a penetrating stare.

'Don't let me down, Alabaster.'

He turned on his heels and disappeared down the spiralling walkway, as quickly as Alabaster was whisked away by Kobold and Nixie, back into the dark bowels of the building.

Twenty-Eight

MARY'S NEW CLOTHES

In the basement, the elves were busy at work. An enormous machine in the centre of the room spat out pieces of pine wood for chopping, sawing, sanding and painting. The monstrosity's mechanical hissing and chugging was punctuated only by the clicking of Nixie's staff against stone as she sauntered around the factory floor, supervising the elves' activity.

Mary, still wearing the clothes she had arrived in, was feeling distinctly uncomfortable. The work was strenuous and brought forth a sweat, each trickle of perspiration disappearing into the folds of yesterday's underwear, her sleeves clinging to her arms like they had been undercoated with super-glue. To make matters worse, her shoulder was beginning to hurt from all the sawing. Stretching her arms above her head to ease her aching muscles, she couldn't help but wince at the unpleasant odour that wafted up to her nostrils – the unpalatable scent of clothes more than two days old.

Mary offered a dainty wave as Nixie passed by officiously on the opposite side of her workstation.

'Excuse me, may I speak with you?'

The Wild Elf looked distinctly unamused. 'What is it?'

'Is there any chance I might be able to get a change of clothes?'

Nixie blinked in astonishment. 'Might I remind you this is a toy shop, not a department store?'

'But my suitcase got lost on the way here.'

Nixie snapped with a sarcastic sneer, 'Isn't that too bad?'

The snarl on her lip prohibited Mary from offering a response – Nixie was not somebody anyone would volunteer to upset. Mary tried to think of what to say, but it was the occupant of the stool beside hers who finally broke the silence.

'You can borrow one of mine,' she said. It was Needles's sister, Holly. She had stopped her work to listen, as – apparently – had all of the other elves within earshot of their conversation.

Nixie shrugged. 'I'm afraid not. The suitcases have been removed for safe-keeping.'

A glance around the room confirmed that it was true. The suitcases were nowhere to be seen.

'But these clothes are just awful,' Mary said, overcome with impatience. 'They're starting to smell, and not in my usual pleasingly fragrant way. In fact, I'd wear that potato sack over having to keep these on a moment longer.'

'Oh, really?' Nixie's mouth puckered in thought.

'Really,' Mary said. 'I don't know if Mr Bandersnatch is aware, but these conditions are a clear breach of the Geneva Convention.'

Nixie eyed the crumpled potato sack on the floor and looked back at Mary. 'Whatever princess asks for, princess shall get.'

She raised the end of her staff and gave it a violent shake. In a flash, Mary found herself wrapped inside the rough, unflattering fibres of the potato sack. Beside her, her empty dress crumpled to the floor.

'And princess will be grateful for it.'

Mary gazed down aghast at her new attire, the sharp fibres prickling her skin. 'But this… this is outrageous!'

'We'll say no more about it,' said Nixie.

Mary was about to give Nixie a piece of her mind, when a low hum began to emit from the end of her staff, which now glowed a luminescent emerald, drawing Mary's gaze like a moth to a flame.

'Princess is grateful,' said Nixie.

'Princess is grateful,' Mary repeated tonelessly.

'Princess won't complain any longer.'

Mary repeated the words.

'Princess will do as she's told.'

Twenty-Nine

CORNELIUS'S BARGAIN

Alabaster paced his umpteenth circuit around the workroom carpet, all the while tapping the rubber-end of his pencil like a steady drum roll against the cover of his notepad. It would take next to no time to produce the designs that Cornelius required; having already fashioned several versions of the snurfer already, he knew the intricacies of its design as well as he knew his own face. And yet, Santa's words echoed inside his mind like an insistent, unwelcome melody.

Humans must never be exposed to magic.

With a weary sigh, he plopped back down onto his stool. He wished he were more motivated. But, with Santa's warnings ringing in his ears, it felt impossible.

His disobedience had already caused so much damage.

Were humans to ever get their hands on elfish magic, their first instinct would be to use it against one another or, worse, against us.

He could not imagine Cornelius intentionally harming anyone. He was, after all, the one who had given Alabaster the opportunity to fulfil his dream.

Rules exist for a reason, Alabaster.

Perhaps he could somehow persuade Cornelius not to begin production of the snurfer; perhaps he could persuade him to choose one of his other designs. Yes! He had notebooks full of ideas: boomerang gliders, voice-activated robots, ping-pong pistols, rainbow-makers – toys that relied on elvish technology rather than magic. Surely there had to be one that Cornelius would find as appealing.

He snatched up one of his old notebooks and flicked through its pages. All the while, his mind stubbornly returned to the question of how Santa was doing since he and the others had departed the Grotto. He similarly wondered about Mary, and cursed himself for having roused from his sleep too late to see for himself. A loose page detailing his invention for the All-Seeing-Snowglobe fell from the notebook and tumbled onto the floor. As he leant down to pick it up, he was pricked by a pang of nostalgia. What he wouldn't give for one of those right now.

While examining the old volume of ideas, it struck him how much fun it had been creating them. Each pen stroke, each frenzied scribbled line showed the immeasurable pleasure of concocting, puzzling over and building each and every new idea.

All of which been denied by the Grotto's senior panel for one reason or another.

This was his big chance; he was not going to blow it.

There was a knock at the door. Before he had chance to acknowledge it, Cornelius had already waltzed inside.

'How is my little genius doing this afternoon?'

Alabaster forced a smile. 'It's going very well,' he lied. 'I've just been looking through my collection of designs.'

'And the snurfer blueprint, is it done?'

'I was just getting to that.'

Cornelius let out an unimpressed snort. 'What's the delay?'

'None, really. I was just trying to gain some inspiration before getting started. It would be a pleasure to show you some of my other ideas –'

'I'd be only too delighted,' Cornelius said flatly. 'Once the snurfer is done.'

'Of course,' Alabaster said. 'I'm just getting to it.'

Cornelius took a seat opposite Alabaster and offered him a pencil. 'No time like the present.'

A clock on the wall ticked with jagged insistence.

Hiding his reluctance with a nod and the most convincing smile he could muster, Alabaster took the pencil and sat at the work-desk. He tore a large sheet of grey paper from a roll before securing its curled edges to the rim of the desk with bull clips. Under Cornelius's impatient gaze, the drawing took less than ten minutes to complete. He sketched and labelled all the various parts, except the one that Cornelius didn't know about – the levitation powder. Alabaster would leave any mention of it off the design. Without it, a snurfer was no more dangerous than an ordinary sleigh.

Once the sketch was completed, he turned the page toward Cornelius who examined it with beady eyes.

'And the prototype?'

Alabaster shook his head. 'When can I see Mary?'

'Whenever you like, my dear boy,' Cornelius said with a chuckle. 'Just as soon as the work is done.'

'But that's not fair…'

Any trace of humour in Cornelius's manner disappeared at once, his smirk replaced with a withering scowl that chilled Alabaster to the bone. 'You appear to be forgetting who is the boss here, Mr Snowball. Remember it is *I* who is giving you this opportunity, and *I* whom you need to keep happy in order that you don't find yourself replaced.'

Alabaster could not believe what he was hearing. 'Replaced?'

Cornelius rose to his feet and put on his hat.

'I meet with my investors tomorrow at noon. The sooner you get me the prototype, the sooner you will get to see your friend. It is in your own interests to provide me with the prototype at your earliest convenience.'

And then he was gone.

Alabaster sat for a moment, in a daze.

The sooner you get me the prototype…

He got up and went to the cupboard.

…the sooner you will get to see Mary.

He selected a flat slab of wood, carried it to the work-desk and, with renewed diligence, set to work.

Thirty

REVELATIONS

Alabaster had been hard at work for several hours when, from the corner of his eye, he spotted something scuttling across the corner of the room. A mouse, with orange fur and pink ears and a long, worm-like tail.

He ignored it at first, persevering with the task at hand, twisting a stubborn screw into a slab of wood. As he continued, the mouse emerged from the safety of the skirting and scuttled directly towards him, its whiskers twitching with interest. Alabaster stopped what he was doing and set down the half-completed snurfer on the workbench. The mouse came closer still, until it stood an arm's length away. It stood on its hind-legs and sniffed at the air.

'Well, hello little guy.'

He reached out a finger, but the mouse darted away. Perhaps he had frightened it? To Alabaster's surprise, it stopped to peer back at him over its shoulder, before continuing on its path towards the door.

'You want me to follow you?'

Alabaster pursued close at its tail, observing its every move with great curiosity. He didn't speak Mouse, but had an unshakeable suspicion that the creature was trying to communicate with him. In the shadows of the doorway, two pairs of oversized feet appeared. He raised his gaze to come eye-to-eye with Kobold. Nixie, standing beside him, fumed. The end of her staff emitted an emerald glow.

The mouse let out a petrified squeak before scampering along the skirting and disappearing through the door behind them.

'Going somewhere?' Nixie's penetrating glare made Alabaster cringe with guilt, even though he had done nothing wrong.

'Oh, no-nowhere. I just thought I saw a –'

Nixie raised an eyebrow.

'– a shadow.'

Kobold's ever-suspicious gaze swept the room as he stepped inside, his clever eyes absorbing every nook and cranny for a detail out of place. While Kobold's eyeballs were otherwise occupied, Alabaster snatched up the maroon box from the worktable and quietly stuffed it into the sack. 'How is work coming along?'

Alabaster held up the half-completed snurfer. 'The prototype is almost done.' Kobold took it and examined it with wide eyes. He looked almost impressed. He set it down on the work-bench and fixed Alabaster with a peculiar stare. 'We're so glad you came to join us, Alabaster.'

'Why, y-yes,' Alabaster stammered. 'Me too. It's – it's quite the honour to work for Mr Bandersnatch.'

Kobold let out a throaty laugh entirely devoid of mirth or merriment. 'That's not what I meant.' He laid a hand on Alabaster's shoulder, his breath hot and sour. 'You're one of us.'

'That's right,' Nixie agreed. 'You're a Wild Elf. Just like us.'

They regarded him strangely.

'Don't say you hadn't noticed,' said Kobold. His crooked smile seemed almost friendly. 'Of all the elves that have joined us, you're the only one who bears our markings. The only one who shares our blood.'

He wished they'd stop staring. Their manner was making Alabaster nervous.

'Wait – you guys are also Wild Elves?' he said, feigning surprise. 'What a small world it is! Gosh, will you look at the time – you know, I have a lot to do here, finishing up the prototype for Mister Bandersnatch, I really ought to get on with it…'

'Where are you from, Alabaster?'

'I really can't say,' Alabaster said.

'Why not?'

'That is, I don't actually know. I was only a wee tyke when Santa found me all that time ago… I don't remember anything of it. I really couldn't tell you where or why or how. After all, it has been eighty-seven years.'

Kobold and Nixie stopped in their tracks, thunderstruck.

'What is it?' Alabaster said.

They exchanged a startled look. For the first time since having met them, a trace of emotion cracked through Nixie's stony exterior, a glimmer of melancholia flashing behind her eyes.

'Eighty-seven years ago, exactly to the day,' she said, as though in a trance, 'in the wildlands of Oslo, we lost our only son.'

'We had given up hope that he would ever be found,' Kobold said. He stepped forward and put his hand on Alabaster's shoulder. 'Until now.'

Thirty-One

FAMILY TIES

'Auf, is it you?'

Alabaster blinked back and forth between the elves'
faces. The more he looked, the more he realised his own
features bore closer resemblance to theirs than he had
previously noted.

He did not know what to say. Finally, the words
came of their own accord:

'You named me Oaf?'

'Not Oaf,' said Nixie, '*Auf*.'

Kobold lifted his hand, 'You were named after your
mum's grandfather. It means *changeling*.'

'Changeling?'

'You really don't remember a thing, do you?'

Alabaster shook his head.

'Where we come from, amid the wildlands of Oslo,' Nixie said, 'we used to share our mountain with our closest neighbours – the Trolls. Now, being part Troll ourselves, I won't hear a bad word said against them. But I'd be lying if I said things didn't sometimes get a little complicated. You see, while the arrangement was mostly peaceful, the Trolls had some peculiar ways. For instance, they believed it more respectable to be raised by humans than by their own kind, and would seize upon any opportunity to give their own children a human upbringing.'

'What kind of opportunity?' Alabaster asked.

Kobold gave him a serious look. 'It usually meant that an unattended newborn human would be kidnapped, and replaced with an infant Troll.'

Kidnapped? The pain and loneliness of a lifetime of separation was one Alabaster knew only too well; in fact, the more he considered it, the more intense was the pain that gripped him. What evil to deliberately do such a thing. 'That's awful,' he said.

'Not at all.' Nixie gave a shrug of her mountainous shoulders. 'It is not unusual for the Changeling to forget they were ever a troll, and go on to live with their host families forever. You'd be surprised just how many human parents don't even notice a switch has taken place.'

Alabaster found that very hard to believe.

'What happens to the kidnapped human babies?'

'Perhaps we oughtn't dwell on this too much… the point is, we are your family.'

'Is that what happened to me?'

'No.'

'Then why are you telling me this?'

Kobold sighed, regarding Alabaster with the haunted look of one who bore the weight of a dreadful secret. 'You were named after your grandfather, who *was* a Changeling. At least, the human infant that had been switched for one. Your great-grandfather was a human.'

Alabaster was flabberghasted. 'You mean…?'

Nixie nodded. 'We're as wild as Wild Elves can be, son.'

In the course of Alabaster's life, it had been difficult enough carrying the burden of being both elf and troll, and tolerating the mean comments from regular elf-folk. But he now had *actual human* in the mix? He felt disgusting; soiled, somehow.

It certainly explained a lot. About how deeply he felt things. About how making the right decision seemed to be always so incredibly hard. The human experience was known, even to elf-folk, for being fraught with difficulty. Now to discover that he too had been cursed with it from birth – it was a lot to take in. But there was still so much he was burning to know.

'All that time ago, what happened? Did you abandon me?'

The gaze of Nixie's dark eyes seemed to see straight through him. 'You ventured out one day and never came back. Christmas Eve, it was. Word got around that you'd wandered beyond the perimeter.'

That certainly sounded like Alabaster.

'We assumed you couldn't find your way back to us.'

'That must have been when Claus found you,' said Kobold, 'and took you to the Grotto.'

Alabaster's eyes flicked from face to face. He did not know what to do. He certainly did not feel like participating in the family hug that such an occasion might ordinarily warrant.

He had an idea.

He took a step back, regarding his new Wild Elf family with scepticism. 'You say you're my family...? You say families owe each other loyalty...'

The two exchanged a private look. Kobold returned his gaze to Alabaster with narrowed eyes. 'Go on.'

'Take me to see Mary.'

The two rose to attention at once, any trace of softness instantaneously evaporating. 'Your request is denied.'

'If you had any love for me at all,' Alabaster said, 'you would know how much this means to me.'

'Who said anything about love?' Nixie gave a snort. 'Our loyalty is to Mr Bandersnatch. As is yours.'

163

'You have one objective here,' Kobold said, 'and that is to complete your duties to Mr Bandersnatch's satisfaction. And stay out of trouble.'

Before following Nixie out of the door, Kobold turned to look at Alabaster.

'I look forward to building a relationship with you, son.'

And they were gone.

Alabaster blinked after them.

It was the strangest thing. The one thing he had longed for all his life now seemed unreal, and not altogether as appealing as he had imagined. Revolting, even. The reunion certainly hadn't raised the feelings he thought it would. He had imagined it would mean he finally belonged. Instead, it felt like he was now expected to comply with whatever they should ask of him. He strongly doubted that they would ever offer the same courtesy in return.

Loyalty. Alabaster scoffed.

Eager to turn his attention to something else, anything, he picked up the half-completed prototype and continued with his work.

High above him, perched on one of the shelves, an orange-coloured mouse watched as he worked long into the night.

Thirty-Two

BREAKFAST STEW

Mary awakened to the sound of a metal saucepan being beaten with a ladle. The cacophony echoed around the walls of the enormous chamber and rang inside Mary's head like she had swallowed an alarm clock.

'Breakfast is served, ladies,' Nixie barked.

In the bunk above her own, a bulging mattress whined as its occupant stirred. Mary drowsily sat up and, wrapped in a cotton bed-sheet, turned her legs over the side. They prickled with goosebumps at the bitter draught that blasted through the workroom. Reluctantly, she retrieved the potato sack from the floor, pulled it over her body and joined the other elves lining up at the food trolley, where Nixie was ladling food from a pot into shallow, ceramic bowls.

The lumpy, grey-brown mixture was unidentifiable. 'What is that?' Mary asked when it was her turn to be served.

'Stew.'

'For breakfast?'

'It's breakfast stew.' Nixie shrugged her shoulders and tilted her head aggressively. 'Like it or lump it, sweet cheeks.'

Without further comment, Mary took the bowl and went to sit at a nearby table, where another group of elves were congregated. Silently, they dipped their spoons into their bowls, mechanically shovelling its contents into their mouths.

'Please. Eat.'

Mary looked at the concoction, and felt her mouth water – not the kind when you feel hungry, but the kind of thick saliva that happens before you throw up. Then her hand dropped the spoon into the bowl's watery contents, and she slurped hungrily at the mixture. It tasted as foul as it looked, with the texture of shredded cabbage and the aroma of weeks' old socks. Once again, her hand dropped the spoon into the bowl and lifted it to her mouth, as though she were a marionette controlled by a puppeteer.

An unidentified piece of meat, tough and tasteless as leather, together with lumps of gristle and cartilage, became lodged in her teeth. If she had wanted to spit it out, she couldn't. Again and again, her hand dropped the spoon into the food and lifted it to her lips until there was nothing left.

Once she was done, a sharp pain stabbed in her abdomen, accompanied by a noisy squirming sound. The spoons of the elves around her continued to clink as they dipped mechanically into their bowls.

Over the tannoy, jaunty Christmas music continued to play.

Thirty-Three

A SLIGHT CHANGE OF PLAN

The last lick of paint applied, Alabaster stepped back to admire his handiwork. Not too shabby, if he did say so himself. Of all the snurfers he had crafted by hand so far, this was by far the best and most handsome-looking. It seemed the more that he made, the better they were.

Most importantly of all, its completion meant that he would finally be allowed to see Mary.

Noon, Cornelius had said. Unable to bring himself to wait for another hour, Alabaster bundled the snurfer into a sack and put on his shoes.

'No time like the present,' he said under his breath, allowing himself a secret smile.

As he was about to open the door, he froze. There it was again.

The mouse.

Had it been waiting for him?

He heaved the door open. The mouse dashed out onto the stairwell and turned to scurry down the stairs. When Alabaster didn't follow, it stopped and turned to look.

'No, this way!' Alabaster hissed. 'We have to go up.'

The mouse let out an angry squeak and continued to descend the stairs.

Dumb mouse.

No sooner had Alabaster turned to climb the staircase than he was astonished to see the rodent scurry between his feet and up several of the steps ahead, stopping at eye level. Arms raised with apparent urgency, the mouse squeaked angrily, as if it were shouting at him.

'What are you playing at?' Alabaster reached out to try and calm the animal with a stroke beneath its chin. To his surprise, the mouse nipped the end his finger with its chipped front teeth.

'Ow!' Alabaster howled. 'What was that for?'

At once, the mouse scuttled back through his legs down a handful of stairs, before turning and squeaking in such a manner that Alabaster felt glad he didn't speak

Mouse. Then it disappeared down the stairs into the gloom of the basement.

Crazy animal.

Alabaster looked at the shadows above him at the top of the stairwell. The sooner he gave Cornelius the prototype, the sooner he would get to see Mary.

With the sack containing the snurfer and the Naughty List clutched tightly in his fist, he made his way up to Cornelius's office.

Thirty-Four

WILHELMINA TURNPIKE

At the second from the topmost floor, Alabaster pressed his ear to the door; Cornelius's unmistakeable tone rumbled from within. It was now or never. Steeling his nerves, he pulled the handle and let himself in without a sound.

He found himself inside a small, dusty room, filled to the ceiling with piles of cardboard boxes bursting at the seams with official-looking papers and folders. A single shard of light poured through a gap in a red curtain that separated the space from the neighbouring room where Cornelius was speaking.

'…in order to maximise our quarterly profits,' he was saying, 'the first, of course, is to eliminate our chief competitor, which – I am delighted to say – we have managed to accomplish.'

On tip-toes, Alabaster skulked towards the curtain and teased it back an inch so that he could get a peek at what was going on.

Cornelius was standing in front of a chart, waving a stick along a red line which zig-zagged up and down like a jagged mountain range. Around the table in front of him were more than a dozen individuals in suits, whose grey pallor suggested they had never been kissed by the light of the sun.

'You mean to say...' one of them ventured.

'Yes, gentlemen,' Cornelius grinned proudly. 'It has taken an incredible amount of planning and perseverance, but I am delighted to announce that the season of freebies and give-aways is no more. The happiest season of all is ours for the taking!'

The assembly burst into wild applause, hooting and hollering with child-like rapture.

'Of course, I couldn't have done it all on my own.' He gestured to a woman seated amongst them, clad in green with ivory-rimmed glasses.

'Please give a warm hand for my wonderful press secretary, Wilhelmina Turnpike!'

Wilhelmina Turnpike? Alabaster was sure he recognised that name...

Cornelius led the applause as the lady, squat and po-faced, stood up and made her way to where he had been standing, her head barely bobbing above the surface of the table. She stood before the screen and pressed a remote-control button. A cosy picture of a traditional Christmas living room appeared, resplendent with glimmering decorations.

'How many among us,' she began, 'remembers the feeling of going to bed as a child on Christmas Eve? The excitement, the restless anticipation? The vivid dreams bearing mountains of gifts? And who here is able to recall the feeling of awakening Christmas morning to nothing but crushing disappointment? To find that, instead of a mountain of presents, Santa has left you nothing more than a piece of coal in your stocking?'

Several hands, including Cornelius's, shot emphatically into the air.

'Who amongst us can admit to having experienced the humiliation of being left with nothing, while all of our goody-goody so-called friends received every precious thing their hearts desired?'

Again, the hands shot up.

'Some say it is punishment for "bad behaviour". Some say it is karma. I say it is nothing more than cruelty of the highest order! And this man is to blame!'

She clicked the button in her hand, and a hideously deformed face in a red winter hat appeared, with a sharp nose and pointed teeth.

'The man they affectionately call *Father Christmas*.'

The woman sneered the name with such unrestrained hatred that Alabaster felt a chill run up his spine. The image, with its grotesque distortions, looked nothing like the Santa that Alabaster knew and loved. Nonetheless, it was met with a chorus of boos and jeers from the besuited individuals around the table.

'This year,' she continued, 'things are going to be different. This year, everyone is going to feel the disappointment. This year, gentlemen, *we get even!*'

As her thundering voice soared to a climax, the room exploded with enthusiastic applause. Quietening them with a slicing gesture, Wilhelmina Turnpike continued:

'So... how does one dismantle this man's power over our lives? How does one take one of the most universally cherished figures of our time and turn him into a figure of hatred and contempt? Easy.'

She pressed the button again, her lips twisted in a crooked smile. A selection of newspaper headlines flashed on the screen, their bold capital letters screaming from the tops of front pages:

SANTA: MIRTH-MAKER OR MENACE?', 'HE KNOWS WHEN YOU'VE BEEN SLEEPING: SANTA'S SINISTER SURVEILLANCE SECRETS', 'SAINT NICK/KRIS KRINGLE/SANTA CLAUS – WHAT THE MULTIPLE ALIASES OF FATHER CHRISTMAS

MEAN AND WHY IT MATTERS' and, most unpleasant of all: *'CHRISTMAS TURKEY: WHY SANTA NEEDS TO GET STUFFED!*

'We tell the truth.'

Gushing with admiration, Cornelius leapt to his feet and led the room in rapturous applause as she returned to her seat. When the ovation subsided, he once again took up the mantle:

'And now, gentlemen, now that the seeds of doubt have been sown, the stage is set for the *pièce de résistance*. It gives me the greatest of all pleasures to unveil possibly my greatest invention yet. I call it: Cornelius Bandersnatch's Splendiferous Snurfboard!'

At a push of the button, the image on the screen changed once again, to reveal a hand-drawn image of the snurfer – the very same that Alabaster had produced only the day before.

He could not believe what he was seeing; Cornelius was claiming Alabaster's invention as his own. Alabaster silently fumed.

'A snowboard?' said one of the men, looking underwhelmed.

'Oh, no,' Cornelius grinned, savouring the drama of divulging a top-secret revelation. 'Not just any snowboard. A *hovering* snowboard. Tell me, what child in their right mind would be able to refuse a ride on a board laced with actual elf magic?'

His hand landed on the table with a loud thud. The congregated audience jolted with shock.

'Just picture it: Christmas morning, when children across the country, across the *globe*, see that their precious gift-bringer isn't so much of a saint after all. What are they to do? Then, all of a sudden, through their television screens they see the announcement: the launch of Cornelius Bandersnatch's Splendiferous Snurfboard, sold exclusively at this very toy shop – the only toy shop in the country that will be open on Christmas Day!'

The boardroom burst into rapturous applause.

'There are three and a half million children in this country alone,' Cornelius continued, his wicked eyes glinting with delight. 'I make that three and a half million disappointed consumers just itching to get their hands on this season's must-have item. Multiply that by the retail price, and gentlemen...' A very large number flashed across the screen. '...we are certain to make this our most profitable Christmas on record.' There was much backslapping and handshaking as Cornelius's audience celebrated their good fortune. 'This year it is I, and not that judgemental old do-gooder, who will be crowned the undisputed King of Christmas!'

At that moment, Alabaster felt a tight grip seize his arm.

'Well, what do we have here?'

It was Kobold. Holding Alabaster firmly in his grip, with his free hand, he pulled back the curtain.

'Sorry to interrupt, Mr Bandersnatch, sir... but it seems we have an intruder.'

Thirty-Five

CORNERED

Silence fell upon the room. A thunderstruck Cornelius looked right at him.

'Well, well, gentlemen,' Cornelius said, in a sneering voice that was unnervingly calm and even. 'It seems we have a spy in our midst.'

Nixie took hold of Alabaster's other arm and the two Wild Elves marched him into the middle of the boardroom. No matter how much Alabaster struggled against their hold, he was no match for their combined strength. The room's inhabitants goggled at him.

'I wasn't expecting you for another hour, Mr Snowball. Just how long have you been eavesdropping, hmm? You naughty sausage.' He let out a condescending laugh that made Alabaster's blood turn to lava.

'I heard everything!' he scowled defiantly. 'You'll never get away with this.'

'And who's going to stop me?'

The first thing Alabaster had to do was to tell the other elves everything he had heard; there was no way they would stand for it if they knew the truth. Just as soon as he was free, that's exactly what he would do.

Cornelius scanned him up and down, his eyes stopping at Alabaster's belt.

'What do we have here?' With a single swipe, he snatched up the deerskin pocket.

'Give that back!' Alabaster cried.

Cornelius smiled and untied the string. The pocket fell open to reveal the sparkling golden-white crystals.

'Unless I'm much mistaken, that's levitation powder, that is,' said Kobold. 'The same levitation powder Santa uses on his sleigh.'

'Of course,' Cornelius said with a smirk. 'You appear to have neglected to mention that in your design, haven't you, Mr Snowball?'

In a single swift motion, he knotted the pocket's drawstring before depositing it in a drawer beneath the table. He glowered at Alabaster through narrowed eyes for a moment.

'Leave him,' Cornelius said.

At once, Kobold and Nixie released him from their

grip and retreated to separate ends of the boardroom, blocking the entryways at either end. Alabaster may have gained the use of his arms, but he was exposed and helpless nonetheless. There was no escape. Unless...

The window! If he could somehow break through to the fire escape on the other side, he might stand a chance... He even had the perfect means to fly away and summon Santa's help. The snurfer was right there. It was worth a shot.

'I brought the prototype you asked for,' he said finally.

'Oh, goody,' Cornelius oozed. 'Where is it?'

Alabaster pointed to where he had left it, lying beside the curtain. 'It's in my sack,' he said.

Before he could make a move towards it, Cornelius seized control of the situation. 'Kobold, would you please?'

Kobold trundled across to the room to retrieve the burlap sack. He presented it to Cornelius, who opened its neck and reached deep inside, before shaking it with a frown.

'Well,' he said, blinking at Alabaster. 'Where is it?'

'What do you mean?' Was this some sort of trick? He had definitely put it inside the sack.

'See for yourself,' Cornelius said, and tossed it to him. He looked inside. It was completely empty. The box containing the naughty list had also disappeared.

Cornelius towered over him with the look of a bull taunted with a red rag.

'You mean to say you've spent all this time and produced nothing?' His words came dangerously slow and quiet.

'I put it inside before bringing it up, I swear!' Alabaster said.

'You're lying!'

'You saw it!' Alabaster said, appealing to Kobold. Ignoring him, Kobold's hands squeezed around Alabaster's arms, once again holding him firmly in place.

'Let me go!'

Cornelius shook his head. 'Oh, no. No, my boy. I can't have some errant spy going around revealing our secrets. That would be bad for business.' He leered dangerously at Alabaster before turning to his assistant with a dark smile. 'Nixie, would you be a dear?'

'It would be my pleasure,' she said. The end of her staff hummed strangely as its luminous emerald hue grew in intensity.

Alabaster was trapped.

'Are you going to kill me?'

'Oh, no dear.' Nixie let out a hearty chuckle that made her whole body shake. 'What sort of mother would that make me? What I can do is ensure you won't be any more trouble. What do you think, Mr Bandersnatch? I think a rat would be most appropriate, don't you?'

'Yes, a dirty, stinking rat,' Kobold agreed.

'No,' Cornelius said, before humming thoughtfully. 'Those big old Wild Elf hands can still be of use to us. Clear his memory.'

'As you wish, Mister Bandersnatch.' Nixie tilted the tip of her staff to Alabaster's face. He screwed his eyes tight shut, not daring to look at the orb of dancing green light, now just inches from the end of his nose. 'There's no use fighting it, Alabaster,' she said. 'Relax. I promise you, you won't feel a thing.'

The tip of the staff, icy cold, pressed against the middle of his forehead.

Terrified, Alabaster let out a scream that echoed around the boardroom's high walls.

Then, all at once, the room fell deathly silent.

Thirty-Six

KRAMPUS RETURNS

Alabaster opened his eyes to find the room in freeze frame; not a soul dared move, every eyeball transfixed upon a monstrous creature that now inhabited the room.

The krampus had returned.

It stood motionless in the centre of the room, fires of fury blazing in its black eyes. Its long, tufted tail flicked back and forth like the head of an aggravated cobra.

Beside it lay the discarded burlap sack.

The steady chink of cloven hooves against the tiled flooring rang out as the creature made its way towards him.

'It's the krampus!' Kobold cried, aghast.

The creature raised its head and glared at Cornelius, who cowered in terror at the opposite side of the desk. Its nostrils twitched as it snorted out a jet of hot air, followed by a bray so loud and shrill that the glass windows shuddered and cracked. The desk's occupants scattered and scrambled for cover, diving behind plant pots and curtains to hide themselves as best they could.

Springing on powerful hind legs, the krampus launched itself onto the desk in a single swoop. It towered over Cornelius, now leaning as far back into a leather chair as its springs would allow.

'Get him!' snarled Cornelius.

He seized the staff from Nixie's hand and turned it, pointing it directly at the creature. Suddenly, a fireball of emerald green exploded from the end, narrowly missing the krampus's head as it ducked. The creature leapt from the desk onto the floor, tiles cracking under the impact of its enormous body. It stretched out a claw and snatched Alabaster up, then tore across the room, Alabaster a mere rag doll in its grip.

'Let our son go!' shrieked Nixie. 'Or you'll be fried to a frazzle!'

Panic-stricken, the creature seized the burlap sack with its free claw and scratched clumsily at the opening. Finally, the mouth of the sack gaped open. Alabaster gazed inside with astonishment. At the bottom was a swirling pool of red and black that looked like volcanic lava.

A second green fireball struck its target; the krampus arched its back and let out a roar of pain. A bald patch of pink skin appeared in the small of its back; tufts of hair, singed and blackened, fringed the edges.

Before he had time to do or say anything, Alabaster was bundled inside.

The last thing he heard Cornelius say was, 'Destroy them!'

Then came the sickening, tumbling sensation as his falling body hurtled down, down, down, while the red-black pool grew ever larger and hotter.

Alabaster closed his eyes, and surrendered to the certainty that he was going to die.

Thirty-Seven

THE UNDERWORLD

Alabaster landed with a thump, the wind knocked out of his body. The sandy ground between his fingertips had the scorched, powdery texture of ashes. As he pulled himself up, his nostrils were hit by a noxious stench of sulphur.

He gazed around to find he was enclosed within the bowels of an enormous infernal cave, the likes of which he might have seen in his darkest nightmares. High above, stalactites of rock dislodged from the roof and plunged into fiery pools beneath, great flames leaping skyward in fountains of orange and yellow, devouring each falling rock with a satisfied gulp.

It appeared he had landed in the centre of a volcano.

Suddenly, a great circle of electric blue light appeared in mid-air and the krampus came hurtling through it like an open doorway. It landed beside him on the soft ash with a thud. Its hindquarters kicked and flailed as it turned itself upright, the sack firmly clutched in its claw.

'What is this place?' Alabaster wondered out loud.

He stood up and looked out upon the expanse of crimson dunes of sand and rock before them, the atmosphere so dense with smog that everything as far as the eye could see was enveloped in a thick cloud of grey. Around them, pools of liquefied rock bubbled and hissed as pockets of escaping gas rose to the surface, each one loaded with that revolting smell. Above them, tendrils of solid rock stretched like the tentacles of a petrified octopus, reaching from one section of the path to another. Beyond that, nestled high within the cavernous roof, a mysterious swirling cloud loomed; a familiar grey whirlpool of smoke with forks of lightning leaping across its shimmering, puddle-like surface.

Through its centre, Alabaster could see the star-spangled moonlit skies of Lapland. For minutes, he gazed longingly upward at the clear, unpolluted atmosphere, before shedding a tear of despair to realise there was no way he would ever be able to reach it.

He found a rock to rest against, and then did not move for several hours.

He had ruined everything.

His entire community was now in mortal danger. It was all because of him.

Idiot.

Worst of all, he was powerless to set it right.

While the little elf sat and stared listlessly into the ashes, sweat drenched his brow, beads pouring out of him like marbles. The creature, meanwhile, was giddy with excitement. Despite its size, it frolicked in the sand like an excited dog. It even brought Alabaster presents in an apparent attempt to cheer him up or engage him in a game of fetch – with zero success, but that did not stop the creature from trying.

Eventually, the krampus ran off again and returned with a new object clamped in its jaws. It dropped at Alabaster's feet.

Alabaster blinked. Could it be? Trembling, he reached out to examine the maroon box.

It was! The very same box that Santa had entrusted to him what seemed an eternity ago.

The scroll was still inside.

And of absolutely no use to him now. Glumly, he sat and unrolled the parchment. His name was still there and, beside it, his ever-growing list of misdemeanours.

He let out a cry of exasperation.

If he had known, he would never have done it. None of it. He only wished that there was some way to turn back time – but there wasn't.

Besides, whatever misdeeds he may have committed, it was surely nothing compared to those carried out by the evil toy-maker on any ordinary Wednesday, before he had even had breakfast.

A thought struck him. With frantic fingers, he unravelled the scroll until he finally found what he was looking for. There it was, in luminous golden lettering: *Cornelius Bandersnatch.*

His hands trembled as he read. A list of no less than one hundred deeds accompanied the toy-maker's name, a catalogue of wicked misadventures that Alabaster could never have begun to imagine, detailing the toy-maker's exploits from early childhood right up to the present day.

It seemed that Cornelius's feud with Santa had been going on for some time. At five years old, he had kicked a department store Santa in the shin in retaliation for gifting him the wrong-coloured yo-yo. At six, he had penned a letter to Santa, threatening to torpedo his sleigh with a land-to-air missile if he did not fulfil the wishes of his Christmas list. The following year, Santa received a mince pie laced with laxatives. Retribution, it seemed, for having received the previous year nothing more than a single lump of coal from the fireplace.

Alabaster's blood curdled as he continued to read through Cornelius's myriad crimes. The man was evil through and through. He had become even more twisted as he grew older.

Writing and publishing news articles intended to destroy Santa's reputation.

Enslaving the elves without their knowledge.

Conspiring to hijack Christmas for personal financial gain...

Something had to be done, and fast! He had the proof. Now he had to tell Santa what was going on.

But how?

Surely, if the naughty list had fallen through the portal into the Underworld, then the snurfer had to be there too. Alabaster sprang to his feet. Fluffy, sensing his renewed excitement, skipped beside him and wagged its tail frantically.

'Where did you find this?' Alabaster said, waving the box under Fluffy's nose. The krampus, as though understanding the little elf's words, turned and bounded out of the cave. Alabaster followed in its tracks along the dunes with all the speed he could muster.

The creature stopped. There, buried in a mound of sand, protruding at a careless angle, was the curved front section of the snurfer. Alabaster retrieved the board from the sand.

'Good boy, Fluffy!'

Thirty-Eight

A SUITABLE LAUNCH-PAD

There was just one problem.

As Alabaster already knew from previous trials, launching the snurfer on flat ground was impossible. Moreover, there was a real danger that any friction from the sand might rub off any remaining levitation powder. Without it, the snurfer would be entirely useless.

There was one thing for it – he would have to find some sort of slope to use as a launch pad.

One of the tendril-like rock formations that protruded from the ground would have to do – its surface, though uneven and narrow in places, appeared to be fairly smooth. However, a single false move or failure to balance correctly along the slope would very likely cause him to topple into one of the pools of lava that bubbled and swirled below, and result in instantaneous death.

Christmas needed saving. There was no time to waste.

Having identified a particular rock formation whose slope was both straight and steep enough, Alabaster hauled the snurfer to its peak and peered down. From below, a geyser of scorching red liquid – several hundred times hotter than boiling water – gushed up towards him. The exploding fountain of lava sprayed huge, deadly droplets all around before sinking again into the pool. A malodorous gust of heat washed over him. Alabaster squeezed his eyes tight shut to stop them burning.

Under any other circumstances, he would have dismissed this as an Appallingly Bad Idea. But it was the best he had.

If he were to survive to tell the tale, the timing would be crucial. He stood on top of the rocky peak, one foot on the board, waiting motionless, poised to begin his descent. A second geyser of lava whooshed up from below. The moment the deadly jet retreated into the fiery pool, Alabaster seized his opportunity and kicked the snurfer into action.

The slope proved not nearly as smooth as he had hoped. Small imperfections along its surface shuddered against the vehicle's wooden underbelly. Keeping control of the snurfer's trajectory proved exceptionally difficult. With alarm, he could feel the board beginning to slide out of control, veering its passenger perilously close towards the edge. Alabaster pulled on the rope with all his might and closed his eyes, silently praying for the best.

Suddenly the shuddering beneath his feet stopped.

Squinting one eye open nervously, he let out an enormous sigh of relief. He had lift-off!

The krampus, now a small black speck against the orange sand below, gazed up at him with wide, astonished eyes. It let out an approving honk that reverberated around the crevices of the cavernous landscape.

'Don't worry, Fluffy,' he cried, 'I'll be back before you know it!'

The little elf steered the snurfboard upwards, in ever-ascending circles until he was directly beneath the swirling vortex. With one last pull on the rope, the snurfer lurched upwards and Alabaster was enveloped inside the eye of the cloud.

Thirty-Nine

RETURN TO THE GROTTO

Alabaster emerged to find he had returned to the very same spot into which the krampus had plunged itself only a couple of weeks ago.

He was home!

And how sweet it was to behold once again the vast white blanket of pure, undisturbed snow and an inky, indigo sky full of stars. He savoured a deep breath of unpolluted Lapland air before steering the snurfer up the mountainside in the direction of the Grotto.

What he saw when he passed through the dome came as a shock. Abandoned and lifeless, the once-magical village was now a ghost town; not a single fairy light flickered in any of the houses, the enormous, silver moon above its only source of light.

As soon as he landed in the main square, Alabaster called out: 'Santa!' But there was nobody to hear.

He made directly for the Big Chief's private quarters. A single yellow candle burned faintly inside the downstairs window. He rapped hard on the door.

'Santa? Santa!'

There was no response.

Alabaster tried again. 'It's me,' he called. 'There is so much I have to tell you. The toy-maker is a fraud. The others are all in danger. And, worst of all… it's all my fault.'

The door opened, and Alabaster found himself face to face with Bushy Evergreen.

'I suppose you had better come in,' he said coldly, before leading him inside.

❊ ❊ ❊

Inside Santa's living room, there was not a trace of tinsel to be seen. Where a majestic, gloriously decorated tree had once stood now was only a bare wooden floor. It was as if the spirit of Christmas itself had been sucked out of the entire village.

'Where is he?' Alabaster asked.

'He's not here,' Bushy replied. 'What do you have to say for yourself, Snowball?'

Alabaster looked hard at the floor. What *did* he have

to say for himself? He thought he had it all planned – but now the words would not come.

'It was me that took the infinity crystal,' he said finally.

'Go on…'

'And I am so, so sorry, Bushy. I thought I was doing it for the right reasons, but I see now it was reckless of me. I've endangered everyone; Santa, the elves, Christmas itself.'

'Reckless, you say? Downright stupid, if you ask me!' Bushy rubbed at his temples with a frown. 'What do you want me to say, Alabaster?' His usually penetrating voice now sounded resigned and tired.

'That you'll help?' Alabaster implored him. 'Please say you'll help.'

Bushy's face grew incandescent with rage. 'You ignored all of our warnings and imperilled our entire livelihoods, not to mention the small matter of breaking up my family, and now you have the audacity to come to me for help?' His voice crescendoed as he spoke, peaking in a shrill howl. 'You've got some nerve, Snowball!'

Beside the bookcase, a doorway opened, and a shaft of light spilled across the pine floorboards.

'Who's there?' a sleepy voice enquired.

It was Santa. He stood in a crack of light, dressed in blue striped pyjama bottoms, as though he himself were getting ready to sleep on Christmas Eve. Alabaster immediately wanted to run and throw his arms around him, and bury his face in the belly that wobbled like jelly, just the same way he did when just a whippersnapper. But he couldn't.

Something was wrong. The ancient man looked more tired than Alabaster had ever seen.

'I thought I heard voices,' he said finally. 'Hello Alabaster.' He offered the elf a faint smile. The creases of his eyes were absent of their usual jolly crinkle.

'Santa, it's so good to see you!' Alabaster replied. 'Please... you have to help us.'

'I do?'

Alabaster explained, 'Cornelius Bandersnatch is a wicked man. He wants to take over Christmas for himself. When all the children wake on Christmas morning to find no presents have been delivered, he's going to entice all the humans into his shop so that he can profit from them, and crown himself the King of Christmas, and take control of the holidays. He's been planning this for years.'

Santa rubbed his head sleepily. 'Alabaster, do you have any idea of the time?'

'If he gets his way,' Alabaster continued, 'it will destroy your reputation for good. Destroy Christmas! You can't let him get away with it.'

'No-one can destroy what's already gone,' Santa

said. 'Two thousand years of sweat and toil to bring happiness, and this is what it gets you.'

'But you can't pay any attention…'

'Really, Alabaster. If, after doing everything you can to please people, all they do is tear you down in return, then what is the point of it all?'

'But don't you see?' Alabaster exclaimed. 'It's Cornelius that's co-ordinating all of this! It's him that's spreading all these lies about you. I have proof!' He pulled the maroon box from where it was tucked inside his belt and opened the naughty list. 'It's all here, see! Take a look.'

He held the parchment up for Santa to see. The old man examined it for a moment, frowning, before waving it away. He looked Alabaster squarely in the eye. 'There's no easy way of putting it. After all that's happened, I'm afraid I just don't believe in Christmas anymore.'

'Don't believe…?' Alabaster could not understand what he was hearing. 'But you're *Father Christmas*!'

Santa turned his face away.

'I wonder,' said Bushy, stepping forward, 'just how many strikes there are against your name, Snowball. Hm? Stealing the Infinity Crystal. Keeping a *pet*, for goodness sake! Ignoring Santa's strict orders…!'

Tears stung Alabaster's eyes. 'I'll show you,' he said, and rolled the scroll across the length of the floor. 'Here, see for yourself. I have nothing to hide.'

Bushy's eyes scanned the document.

'Please help me,' Alabaster said. 'For Mary's sake too. Yes, it was me that created this mess, but it affects all of us. I truly thought I was doing the right thing. I'd do anything to take it back. Please, help me take it back.'

A small wet star stained the wooden boards beneath him as tear landed on the floor.

'I'm sorry, Alabaster,' Santa said, rising to his feet. 'The damage is done. If Cornelius wants Christmas, he's welcome to it. I hope people appreciate his efforts more than they appreciated mine.'

And with that, he disappeared the way he came.

Forty

AN UNLIKELY ALLIANCE

Alabaster stared helplessly at the door through which Santa had disappeared. What was he going to do now? Without Santa's assistance, he had to try and rescue the others himself. But how?

He collected together the scroll parchment, rolling its handles feverishly before returning it to its box.

'You brought this all on yourself, you know,' Bushy said. Though Alabaster did not look at him, he could feel the old elf's penetrating leer. 'I told you no good was going to come of it, I tried to stop you, but oh no! Of course, you knew better...'

'That's not helpful,' Alabaster snapped. He tucked the Naughty List into his belt and headed for the front door.

'Where are you going?'

'I got us into this mess. I'm going to get us out of it. With or without your help.'

❁ ❁ ❁

It was to be expected that Bushy would refuse to offer any assistance, of course – but to see Santa ravaged of all hope was too much to bear. One thing was certain, if Alabaster was going to snurf the entire way back to London, he would need to replenish his supply of levitation powder. He collected up the snurfboard from beside the front door and headed for the stables, to be greeted by eight antlered heads that poked through the top halves of the doors.

He would have to proceed with caution. On more occasions than he cared to remember, they had given him a taste of their antlers' strength, for nothing more than simply getting too close. As a result, he was now every bit as jittery around them as they seemed to be around him.

Standing on the very tips of his toes, he reached over the top of Dasher's door, unfastened the lock and let himself in. In the corner, a sack labelled 'LEVITATION POWDER' sat slumped amid the hay. Alabaster knelt beside it, opened up a handkerchief and scooped several handfuls of the glistening, golden-white powder inside before securing the end with a toggle.

'How is Mary?' a voice asked.

Alabaster flinched to see Bushy Evergreen standing at the stable door.

'I haven't seen her,' Alabaster said. He fastened the handkerchief tightly at his belt. 'Cornelius separated us as soon as we arrived.'

Bushy's brow knotted in concern. 'Is she ok? Do you know if she's been hurt?'

'I don't know,' Alabaster said. 'He's been keeping her in the basement with all the others the whole time we were there. Now, if you'll excuse me, I have a job to do.'

He flipped the snurfer onto its top in the snow and applied a handful of powder to its surface.

'What is that?' Bushy asked.

Ignoring him, Alabaster continued to apply the powder to the underside of the board.

'Correct me if I'm wrong,' Bushy said, 'but I don't think it's going to be big enough for the both of us.'

Alabaster looked at him in shock. 'The both of us?'

'Well, I can't rely on you to do it all by yourself now, can I?' Bushy said, half-smiling. 'Besides, Mary's family. If she needs help, I have to be there.'

Bushy certainly would not have been Alabaster's first choice of partner. Nonetheless, it was a big operation. And help was help, wherever it came from.

'Very well,' Alabaster said.

He hated to admit it, but Bushy was right. The snurfer had just been large enough carry both himself and Mary. Bushy, however – who was rather more rotund than his niece – was an altogether different kettle of fish.

'What do you suggest?'

'It's already past midnight,' Bushy said. 'Technically, it's already Christmas Eve. If we're going to have any hope of rescuing the others in time, there's only one solution.'

'And what's that?'

He glanced up to see Bushy giving Dasher a pat behind the ears, a thoughtful look on his face.

'The fastest mode of transport known to all elf-kind.'

✿ ✿ ✿

'Have you ever driven reindeer before?' Alabaster asked, tentatively joining him in the sleigh. He had the reins in his hands, ready to go.

'Not for a while –'

'You know how unpredictable they can be.' As Alabaster spoke, he could have sworn Vixen cast him a shady look. Ignoring it as best he could, Alabaster placed the folded burlap sack in the glove compartment for safe keeping, alongside Santa's plentiful stockpile of levitation powder.

Bushy rolled his eyes, trying to maintain the last shred of his dwindling patience. 'Who do you think taught Santa to ride this sleigh, Alabaster?'

'And another thing,' Alabaster said, not really listening, 'where are we going to keep eight reindeer while we go searching in the basement? It's not safe for them to stay up on the roof.'

Bushy lifted his jacket. In his inside pocket, an invisible cube jutted out.

'You have the Infinity Crystal?'

Bushy nodded. 'You were right – they're going to need be hidden from view, we can't put them in danger.'

'I thought that was a serious breach of the rules?'

'Was.' Bushy sighed deeply. 'Look around you, Alabaster.'

Alabaster looked around to see a town without a heartbeat, lifeless and smothered.

'What's the Grotto even worth anymore?'

A tear welled behind his eye. 'So much.'

Bushy sighed. 'Are you at least strapped in properly?'

Reluctantly, Alabaster secured the strap across his lap. 'You're really going to do this?'

A grin of excitement spread across Bushy's face. 'You think I can't manage eight reindeer?' He snapped at the reins, and the thunder of thirty-two hooves against the icy ground filled the air.

'Dash away, dash away, dash away all!' Bushy cried.

The sleigh shuddered into life, the sudden jolt of velocity throwing its passengers backward into their seats. Bushy hooted with excitement. For an elf who normally looked like he had never enjoyed a moment's fun in his entire miserable life, he seemed to be on top of the world.

The sleigh, whose undercarriage – like the hooves of the sky-bound reindeer – was now coated with the fine, golden powder, took to the skies as smoothly as an aeroplane.

As the sleigh's occupants lifted ever higher, the Grotto and its darkened buildings shrank into the distance until it had completely disappeared.

✿ ✿ ✿

At precisely six-thirty on Christmas Eve, Alabaster and Bushy landed on the toy-shop roof.

'At ease,' Bushy commanded, and the eight reindeer dutifully relaxed at their station, harrumphing clouds of warm breath into the night sky.

Alabaster pointed to the familiar entrance beneath the tarpaulin. 'The doorway is right there.'

Bushy steered the sled and the reindeer to the closest thing to a hiding place – behind Cornelius's airship. He removed the invisible box from his pocket and raised an invisible lid. He tipped the box and out rolled the crystal, landing in a purpose-made dimple in the sleigh's dashboard. As he did so, the box that contained it (which, it turned out, was indigo and speckled with stars) appeared in his other hand. When the dashboard cover was clicked shut, both the sleigh and the reindeer attached to it vanished.

'Come on!' he said, gesturing for Alabaster to follow as he dashed for the black double-doors. Alabaster tugged at the cold metal handle, but it refused to budge. It was padlocked and bolted from the inside.

'What now?'

'Is there no other way into the building?' Bushy asked.

Alabaster thought for a moment. Apart from the portal sack, this was the only entrance he had used.

'There must be a front entrance,' Alabaster said, 'but we are likely to be seen.'

Bushy scratched his chin thoughtfully.

'I wouldn't be so sure about that,' he mused. 'Come on!'

Forty-One

BLENDING IN

It was a funny thing, thought Alabaster. The number of hours he had spent wishing he could shrink his broad shoulders, and his arms, and every other part of his himself that set him apart from all the others. Now, as he entered the bustling toy-shop with Bushy standing atop his broad Wild Elf shoulders, draped in an oversized Santa suit, he could finally count it as a blessing.

Bushy Evergreen's insatiable year-round appetite for mulled wine and mince pies had endowed him with a portly belly, and weighed much more heavily upon Alabaster's shoulders than his niece had done. Nonetheless, it made far more sense for the older elf to provide the top half of the humanoid figure that now strutted towards the toy-shop entrance, as his face was far less likely than Alabaster's to be recognised by Cornelius or any of his henchmen.

The suit that concealed them both was the spare that Santa always kept in the sled's glove compartment, in case of emergency. Lessons had been learned since the Explosive Diarrhoea Disaster of 1972 when some rotter had laced one of Santa's minced pies with laxatives. Since then, Santa always knew to keep a spare suit in the dashboard.

The white, fur-lined crack between the buttons through which Alabaster peeped was narrow and fuzzy, white fibres obscuring his view of the last-minute Christmas shoppers that crowded the shop floor.

'Easy now,' Bushy said, speaking discreetly into his front collar so that only Alabaster would hear.

'Do you see the video wall beside the teddy display?' Alabaster called up. 'It's behind there.'

'Ok, keep moving right ahead. Steer left a fraction, just ten degrees or so...'

Alabaster obliged, taking care not to bump into any of the bustling humans that stood in the way.

'That's it, we're almost there.'

As they approached the video wall, Cornelius's enlarged, smiling face appeared on the screen.

'...the only toy-store in the whole of the country to still be open on Christmas Day,' he was saying, and a chill ran up Alabster's spine. 'So, should you awaken this Christmas morning to find Santa has not granted all your wishes, remember Cornelius Bandersnatch will be here to make all your Christmas dreams come true.'

Suddenly, one of the human torsos stepped directly in front of them, and Alabaster ground to a halt. He could see that the person talking to Bushy wore a black uniform that read 'SECURITY' in white, stitched letters. On his belt, at Alabaster's eye-level, he carried a walkie-talkie, handcuffs and a cannister labelled 'Magnum Pepper Spray'. Alabaster held very still.

'...seem a little lost,' the man was saying.

'Not at all,' Bushy replied with a dry chuckle.

'You're not meant to be at the Grotto?'

'The Grotto?'

'Yeah, the Grotto's on the fifth floor. You're here for the filming, right?'

'No, no, no; I'm just here to pick up a couple of last-minute things for my nephew before the big day, you know how it is.'

'Oh, I see.' The man stepped aside. 'Sorry to have bothered you, Sir. Have yourself a very Merry Christmas.'

Once the man had disappeared from view, Alabaster resumed walking at a quickened pace. As he rounded the side of the video wall, he called up to Bushy, 'What was that?'

'A very close call,' Bushy hissed down to him. 'Are we almost there?'

'It should be right about…'

Before he could finish speaking, the tail of the coat caught under Alabaster's feet, and he lost his balance. Bushy tumbled from his shoulders and sprawled head over heels onto the tiled floor in front of them. Around them, shoppers blinked in disbelief at the sight of a peculiar man dressed in a Santa outfit splitting into two.

'Quickly,' Alabaster cried in panic, as he scrambled to his feet, 'RUN!'

Forty-Two

THE BASEMENT

Without stopping to draw breath, Alabaster and Bushy scrambled to their feet and disappeared through the door. A narrow foyer led through a second door and into the stairwell.

They were alone.

'Are you ok?' Alabaster panted. The noise of bustle and Christmas music from the toy shop floor was replaced with an ominous silence, except a steady drip-drip of water droplets falling onto the stone floor below.

'Agh,' Bushy groaned. 'I hit my head.'

'Let me see.'

Bushy lifted his hand to reveal a large, reddened bump on his forehead.

'Do you think you'll be ok?'

With a snort of irritation, Bushy waved Alabaster away. 'It'll take more than a fall to stop me,' he said, before staggering forward and reaching for the metal bannister to maintain his balance.

'Here, let me help you.' Alabaster took Bushy's elbow and led the old elf down two circling flights of steps to the basement floor. Behind a black door, the unmistakable sound of factory machinery chugged and clattered.

'This must be the place,' Alabaster whispered, pressing his hands to the door. It did not give way; instead, his fingers fell upon a large steel padlock.

'We're going to need a hacksaw or something to get through,' Bushy said.

A hacksaw! By Jove, the old elf was right. And Alabaster knew exactly where to find one.

'Bushy Evergreen, you are a genius!' he whispered excitedly, ushering Bushy into the shadows of the doorway. 'Stay here, out of sight. I promise I will be no more than five minutes.'

'Where are you going?'

But Alabaster did not answer. He was already halfway up the flight of stairs, headed for his workroom.

❊ ❊ ❊

212

The workroom remained exactly as Alabaster had left it, his bed unmade and loose sketches and pages of notes littering the surface of his desk.

Everything he owned was in this room, all his belongings, his sketches, his clothes. It would only take a few minutes to throw everything into a suitcase… no, there was no time for that. Everyone was relying on him.

He seized a small hacksaw from where it hung upon one of the workbench hooks and retreated back towards the door.

He had barely made it two steps when a voice behind him made him freeze.

'Well, hello, Alabaster,' the voice purred. 'Looking for something?'

Forty-Three

THE PRODIGAL ELF

'We thought we had seen the last of you,' Nixie continued. 'But alas. The prodigal son has returned.'

Alabaster turned to face them with a smile, his mind racing, his heart pounding.

'Hi, Mum. Hi, Dad.'

The Wild Elves remained motionless, glints of fire burning in their eyes.

'I wasn't planning on staying long, just came to collect a few things I left behind.'

Kobold chuckled darkly. 'We're sure Mr Bandersnatch will have something to say about that.'

Side by side, the pair swooped in his direction, their combined size as wide as a snowplough. There was

214

nowhere to escape, except upwards. Alabaster spun round and hoisted himself up the ladder, scaling the rungs as fast as his little legs would carry him. Finally, he managed to pull himself up onto a shelf, just as Kobold's great arm gave a tremendous swing, knocking the ladder clear off its track and sending it crashing to the floor.

'Traitor!' Nixie spat up at him.

'Hush, now darling,' Kobold said, his voice measured. 'He's a good boy really. Come to Daddy, there's a good boy.'

The ledge Alabaster balanced on also contained an enormous box of construction materials, allowing him very little room. His big feet teetered dangerously over the edge. With the very tips of his fingers, he clung to the side of the box, praying he would not overbalance.

'I thought you were happy here, Alabaster,' Nixie crooned, closing in beneath him. 'You have your workshop, your tools, everything you could wish for, right here.'

She licked her lips with excitement. The flame at the end of her staff grew ever brighter. Meanwhile, her soothing voice, enticing and smooth as caramel, increasingly began to resonate inside his own head, as though it were coming from within.

'Everything I could wish for...' Alabaster intoned.

'That's it,' Kobold cooed, standing open-armed beneath him.

Alabaster seized his chance. He heaved on the box beside him with all the strength he could muster, sending it toppling over the edge and onto the heads of the pair below. Its contents of ball bearings cascaded in waves across the workshop floor, knocking Kobold and Nixie off their feet. As Alabaster leapt down after them, the carpet of tiny silver balls sent him skidding. With a thud, he landed flat on his back, all wind knocked out of him.

A thunderous roar shook the room as Kobold lifted the container and tossed it across the breadth of the workshop, sending it crashing into a wall.

Now might be his only opportunity to escape. Alabaster pelted towards the door, only to find Nixie there before him.

He froze.

'You ungrateful little cockroach,' she fumed. She barged him with her wide frame, sending him tumbling. As she advanced, Alabaster scrambled backwards on his elbows. 'Everything you ever wished for has come true, has it not?' The green glow at the end of her staff pulsated as she spoke, growing brighter with every word. 'Your wildest dreams of becoming an inventor? Your own workshop? Handed to you on a plate! And what do you do? You are a traitor.'

Alabaster had heard enough.

'Cornelius doesn't care about you!' he retorted

defiantly. 'Don't you see? He's using you. He's using all of us. We're not his slaves.'

Nixie laughed coldly. 'And your precious Santa? He's been using you for centuries!'

The back of Alabaster's head met with something hard and cold. A steel dustbin lid clattered to the floor.

He was cornered.

Nixie chuckled. 'An undeserving, treacherous insect like you is no son of mine!' she roared, before pointing the staff – now burning with the fury of a thousand suns – in his direction. In desperation, Alabaster grabbed the dustbin lid and, shielding his eyes from the light, held it in front of his face.

The last thing he saw before squeezing shut his eyes was Nixie's enraged scowl, bathed in the dazzling emerald beam that exploded from the end of her staff.

Forty-Four

KOBOLD'S DILEMMA

The clattering of wood upon a stone floor echoed around the now-silent room.

Alabaster lowered the dustbin lid. Nixie had vanished. In her place, on the floor, a small cockroach lay on its back, its tiny legs wriggling furiously as it attempted to turn itself upright.

'My love!' Kobold screamed, and ran to the spot from which she had vanished.

Upon seeing the squirming cockroach, he let out a roar of fury. The sound of it alone made Alabaster's head spin. Before he could move, Kobold seized the fallen staff and pointed its tip in his direction.

'You!' he growled. 'You did this!'

Alabaster couldn't be entirely sure what had happened. The inside of the dustbin lid was now emblazoned with the smear of a large black scorch mark.

'I… I…' Alabaster stammered, but the words would not come. Kobold's face, incandescent with rage, leered into his.

'I'm going to squish you like a bug!' Kobold roared. The staff pulsated, emitting a steady hum, the shadows from its eerie glare making Kobold's face appear more terrifying than ever.

Then there was silence.

'I can't…' he said. 'Not to my own flesh and blood. Not to the only son I have.'

Alabaster opened his eyes to see Kobold fall to his knees, silently weeping.

Seizing his opportunity to escape, Alabaster leapt to his feet and ran to the door.

The last thing he saw before he fled the workshop room was Kobold's wretched figure crouched on the floor, face buried in hands.

Forty-Five

BUSHY'S COMPANION

When Alabaster arrived in the basement floor, Bushy's face was lit up in the hazy blue glow of his wristwatch light.

'Five minutes, you said,' Bushy scolded. 'It's been seven and a half.'

'I'm sorry, Bushy – I, my parents… There's no time to explain.'

'And the hacksaw?'

The hacksaw.

Alabaster winced. The very thing he had gone there for, he had forgotten.

'I got sidetracked. When I got in there…'

'Shh!' Bushy hissed. 'Don't… move.'

Alabaster turned his gaze in the same direction as Bushy's – bathed in the glow of the wristwatch, watching them intently, was a large rodent.

'A rat!' Bushy whispered. 'There's probably hoards of them down here, ravenous, waiting for just such an opportunity to feast on an elf separated from the others...'

The rodent rose to stand on its hind legs, and Bushy let out a shaky gasp. The creature's whiskers twitched as it sniffed the air, its eyes sparkling with the reflection of Bushy's wristwatch.

'Thankfully, it looks like it's alone,' said Alabaster.

Suddenly, the rodent began to scamper towards them. Bushy drew back in fear, pushing Alabaster's back into the door. The electric blue light died, plunging the space into blackness.

'Turn on the light,' Alabaster said.

'I'm trying,' Bushy whimpered as he fumbled with the buttons.

When the light returned, the rodent was no longer where it had been standing.

'Here, look.' Bushy's finger indicated the base of the door, where the animal was climbing up with its sharp claws. Halfway up, it slowed then stopped, settling just centimetres below the padlock.

'It's no rat,' said Alabaster. 'That mouse has been following me for days. I swear, it's almost like it's been trying to tell me something.'

To his amazement, the mouse swivelled its body around and began to prod at the lock with the end of its long, worm-like tail.

Suddenly, an alarmed squeak rang out as the mouse lost its footing and began to plunge towards the concrete floor.

Reflexively, Alabaster lunged forward and caught it in cupped hands. The trembling mouse let out a squeak.

He lifted the mouse to the level of his eye. The startled animal's heartbeat pounded furiously against his palms. Its long front teeth glinted in the light. One of them, Alabaster saw, bore a chip that looked oddly familiar.

It couldn't be…

Alabaster blinked. 'Needles… is that you?'

The mouse let out an excited squeak and ran in circles around Alabaster's palm.

There was no time to lose. Alabaster held Needles-the-mouse beneath the padlock, and once again it inserted the end of its tail into the lock. A look of rapt concentration crossed its face, a little tongue protruding from the corner of its mouth.

With a click, the lock sprang open.

'You did it!' Bushy exclaimed in triumph, forgetting to keep his voice low.

Alabaster lowered the mouse to the floor and removed the padlock. Without losing a second, Needles had scampered beneath the crack and disappeared into the room on the other side.

'There's only one thing left to do,' said Bushy, as Alabaster pocketed the padlock.

He gently pushed open the door.

Forty-Six

THE FACTORY

Nothing could have prepared Alabaster and Bushy for the sight that greeted them on the other side of the door.

Beneath the cold glare of white fluorescent lighting, the cavernous room looked, to all intents and purposes, like a factory. An enormous machine in its centre chugged and hissed, occasionally spitting out large, flat slabs of wood onto a vast network of conveyor belts that snaked around the centre of the room. An army of worker elves were seated at an endless row of stools alongside the belt. They did not seem to notice the duo arrive at all, so busily focused were they on their work. Perhaps it was their glazed expression, or their oddly mechanical way of moving, but something about the scene reminded Alabaster of characters in a clockwork toy.

Placid music poured in through a speaker high on the wall, a steady drone over which a soft voice soothed a calming mantra: 'Productivity is the root of all happiness. The more you make, the happier you will be. This, after all, is the happiest time of the year, is it not? Think of the happiness your efforts will bring, those bright joyful faces on Christmas morning, the hearts that will sing, and it's all thanks to you. Most of all, please know Cornelius is very happy with you. That should make every one of you very, very happy…'

'Can you see Mary anywhere?' Bushy said, his eyes sweeping the sea of blank faces.

Alabaster looked around. It was so hard to distinguish between them. Except for one of them. One of them was dressed in a potato sack.

'Look, there,' he said, pointing.

'Mary!' Bushy called out.

'Uncle Bushy?' she said, rising to her feet. 'Is that you?'

'It's so good to see you!' He embraced her, but Mary's arms remained stiffly at her side. 'If you're still angry with me, I will understand,' he said. 'I'm just so relieved you're ok. But…' He pointed to her dress. 'What on earth is this?'

225

'This old thing?' She let out a strange mechanical laugh and gave a twirl. 'I lost my suitcase on the journey here, so they kindly gave me this to wear instead.'

Her eyes remained distant and glazed. She seemed not to notice Alabaster's presence at all.

'And this is where you sleep?'

Around the room's perimeter, a metal complex of bunk beds easily ten levels high were piled on top of one another, with steps and ladders leading to the top.

'Yes, isn't it perfect? Everything we need is here, in this room.'

Something was wrong. A white-green orb danced like a firefly in the centre of her pupils. Bushy put his hands on her shoulders and shook her gently.

'Mary, I've come to get you out of here. All of you. We have to leave. Right this minute.'

Some of the elves had now turned to face them, their expressions blank and unreadable. The same green glint shone in all their eyes.

Still the recorded voice continued over the hypnotic musical drone: 'Bandersnatch Toys is the happiest place on earth. Everything you need is here…'

Mary's face wore a bewildered smile. 'Leave?' she said. 'Why on earth would we want to do that? Everything we need is here.'

Forty-Seven

BACK AT THE BASEMENT

The drone of the pre-recorded voice continued, the same words repeating on an endless loop.

'But the Grotto. Santa…'

It was no use. Mary's unblinking eyes smiled back, innocent of any thought other than the task at hand. She returned to her stool and continued with her work.

'We have to round the elves up,' Alabaster said. 'And quickly.'

But how?

Screwing up his courage, Bushy trotted into the middle of the room. To gain everybody's attention, he stomped his foot loudly on the floor.

'Elves, listen up!'

227

Back at the Grotto, this would have been enough to make the elves stand to attention like a troop of soldiers. However, he was dismayed to see no more than a handful look up at the sound of his voice. Just as quickly, those looks turned dismissively back to their work.

'EVERYBODY!'

Still, nobody flinched.

'It's no use. Bushy,' Alabaster said. 'Not over the noise.'

The speaker was positioned high up on the wall. If only there was something to hand that he could use...

At that moment, the machine spat out another slab of wood which slid down the conveyor belt. Before any of the workers could claim it, Alabaster dashed across the workshop floor and into the machinery to retrieve it. He stood on it and pulled with all of his might, snapping it in two. He positioned himself a little away from the wall and tossed the first broken piece in the direction of the speaker. To his disappointment, it missed and clattered miserably to the floor. The worker elves, unresponsive, continued with their duties.

Undeterred, he picked up the second half and flung it like a frisbee in the direction of the speaker.

Success!

The impact knocked the speaker off its fixture and it crashed to the floor. The room fell silent. All of the elves stopped their activity.

At the other end of the room, Bushy puffed himself up proudly. '*Now*, do I have everybody's full attention?'

Every eye turned to look at him.

'Cornelius won't like that,' Crackerjack said, his voice strangely monotone.

Another got to his feet. 'Intruder.'

'But… but, it's your old friend, Bushy Evergreen,' he stammered in panic. 'I'm here to save you.'

'Santa is a criminal,' they intoned, as one. 'He must be stopped.'

A legion of elves bared their pointy teeth.

Bushy was surrounded.

Forty-Eight

DO YOU HEAR WHAT I HEAR?

The sudden silence felt very strange. Like a ringing in Mary's ear had suddenly ceased after days of relentless noise.

She looked at the fallen speaker. Cornelius Bandersnatch was not going to be happy. Of that, she was certain.

Nor, indeed, were the throng of factory elves who had raised themselves from their work-stools and begun to encircle her uncle on the factory floor.

'We have to go up to the roof!' her uncle was saying. 'It's our only chance.'

'Cornelius has not asked us,' Crackerjack hissed. 'Are you asking us to disobey Mister Bandersnatch?'

'Wait,' Alabaster cried. 'You don't understand. I am here to help you!'

The sound of Alabaster's voice rang through the air. Mary blinked in surprise. His voice, she suddenly realised, was the only sound she had wanted to hear since she had been brought to this place. To tell her everything would be ok. To make her laugh. To make her smile. It had felt so, so long that... she had almost forgotten all about him. How could that be? A single tear fell from the corner of her eye and dropped to the floor. She lowered her gaze to see the wet mark of a black star.

With some disgust, she realised that the brown dress she was wearing was not her own. The material was coarse and aggravated her skin, its hard bristles poking into her, all over her body. Around her shoulders, where her arms protruded through the material, were red scratches, fiery and inflamed like a rash.

Mary suddenly felt the urge to scream. Why on earth was she dressed in a potato sack?

✿ ✿ ✿

'Don't hurt him,' Alabaster said, rushing to Bushy's side.

'Look who it is,' said Alvin. 'Nixie warned us to look out for you. The traitor.'

The circle of elves seethed with fury.

'We're your friends,' Alabaster said. 'Remember?'

None of the elves softened. He fished the maroon box from Bushy's coat pocket and fumbled to unroll it.

'Cornelius has been deceiving you,' he said. 'Look!'

He held the open parchment aloft for all to see. For a moment, all eyes were drawn to the scroll.

'This is the naughty list, entrusted to me by Santa. It lays out Cornelius's plot, in full detail. And how he has used us to achieve them. If we let him win, Christmas will be destroyed for ever.'

'We don't have long,' Bushy added. 'We have to escape to the roof while there is still time.'

'Lies!' Alvin screeched. He repeated the word while thumping at his chest, and the elves began to chant along with him until the air was filled with the furious chanting of two hundred angry elves.

Alabaster and Bushy staggered backwards.

'Get them!' Crackerjack cried.

Suddenly, another voice began to echo around the enormous room.

'Cornelius is happy with you,' it said, stopping the elves in their tracks. They stood frozen to the spot as it continued: 'The work you do for the world's children. You should be happy and proud of all that you do in this, the happiest place on earth.'

Alabaster looked around in confusion. What on earth was happening?

'The master feels that all elves deserve to be rewarded for their hard work,' the voice continued. 'The master requests that all elves make their way to the rooftop, immediately.'

Alabaster's eyes landed upon Mary who, crouching behind the assembled throng, held the cracked speaker to her mouth.

'Immediately...' the elves intoned, and began to walk in the direction of the open door.

From across the room, Mary smiled at Bushy and Alabaster. Bushy heaved a sigh of relief.

'That was a close one,' said Alabaster.

Forty-Nine

UP ON THE ROOFTOP

The bracing December night air fell upon Alabaster's cheeks like a blizzard of pine needles. The other elves appeared not to notice the temperature dip at all as they followed him onto the rooftop, their trance having apparently rendered them oblivious to feeling. Mary, on the other hand – whose bare arms and legs were exposed to the elements – began to chatter her teeth like a pneumatic drill.

'Now what?' she asked.

'We have to get them all on board,' Alabaster said, pointing to the enormous airship tethered to a mast at the end of the rooftop.

'Can you drive an airship?'

Bushy stepped forward. 'I served in the Armed Elf Forces during the Elf War of 1937. If anyone would be qualified to try, it would be me.'

'I can make an announcement,' said Mary, 'Just give me the signal.'

Alabaster nodded and they both ran to the airship carriage. Bushy pulled at the door handle, but it was no use.

'It's locked.'

There was only one thing for it. Alabaster retrieved the burlap sack from the reindeer sleigh and pressed it against a glass panel of the under-carriage. He banged hard with his elbow several times, until the pane beneath it shattered with a crack. He reached through the hole and pulled hard at the inside handle.

The door slid open.

Success!

Bushy turned to Mary and gave the thumbs up.

Mary cupped the megaphone to her mouth and, in a calm and mechanical voice, intoned, 'Cornelius Bandersnatch requests that all elves make their way to the airship immediately. All elves, please make your way to the airship.'

Obediently, the elves shuffled in step towards the ship's gondola, where Alabaster took responsibility for ushering them aboard. Meanwhile, Bushy familiarised himself with the cockpit, and its complex networks of levers, buttons and pulleys that operated the vessel.

Crackerjack was the last to come aboard. As he boarded the ship, he stopped and eyed Alabaster suspiciously. 'Where is the master?'

'Don't worry – Cornelius will be here,' Alabaster replied. 'Any minute now.'

He could not have known how right he was.

As soon as the elves had boarded, Alabaster ran to the mast to untether the ship. In moments, Bushy could set sail, carrying the elves to the safety of Lapland.

Suddenly, Cornelius emerged through the stairwell entrance, seething like an enraged bull. The emerald glow of Nixie's cane in his hand pierced the dark like a flare. Kobold followed at his heels.

When he spoke, his voice was a howl of rage. 'Elves, desist!'

Before Alabaster had chance to finish releasing the ropes, the great propellers began to spin and the airship pulled noisily into the air. Tethering cords tautened and snapped, before tumbling uselessly to the ground like dead snakes. The tip of the mast pulled free of its concrete holding, sending a loud crunch to echo through the night air. The ship climbed skyward with the mast's remnants still clinging to its nose.

'No!' Cornelius screamed in panic. 'No, no, no!'

He took aim at the vessel with the end of the staff. A bolt of green fire exploded from its tip and punctured the skin of the balloon with a resounding bang.

Alabaster watched in horror as the airship crashed onto the toyshop roof and rolled onto its side. He ran to investigate the damage when a second green fireball narrowly skimmed past his head and exploded with an ear-splitting roar against a billboard behind him. He stopped in his tracks to see Cornelius pointing the staff at him.

'Fool!' Cornelius's voice boomed, his face contorted with rage. 'Did you really think you could outwit me?'

Suddenly, with the energy of a man half his age, Cornelius raced towards Alabaster. As he did so, he rose high into the air, as though climbing an invisible set of stairs. The soles of his shoes gave off a familiar glimmer. In a single bound, Cornelius leapt over Alabaster's head and landed neatly behind him, gripping him around the neck with the crook of his elbow.

'Don't look so surprised, my little friend,' he sneered, holding Alabaster tightly to his chest. 'You're the one who introduced me to the wonders of levitation powder.'

Grinning, he pointed the tip of the staff at Alabaster's face, the icy heat of its green tip just inches from his nose.

'You've been very useful to me, Mr Snowball. But you have exhausted your usefulness. You seem to have forgotten who's in charge here. All it takes is one word from me, and every single one of your Grotto friends will gladly tear you limb from limb.' A strange smile crossed his face. 'Yes, I think I'd like to see that.'

He pounded the base of the staff on the asphalt roof.

'Elves!' he called. 'I have a little job for you.'

Immediately, the toppled carriage came alive with protruding limbs as elves scrambled to hoist themselves through its broken doors and windows. The spectacle was like a scene from a horror movie, with grunting zombies rising from their graves.

Before Cornelius could give the approaching throng further instructions, Alabaster sprang backwards with all the strength his thick legs could muster and toppled the old man to the ground. The staff flew from his hand and rolled across the asphalt. Cornelius let out a strangled gasp as Alabaster landed on top of him, pinning him to the roof.

The staff! He had to get hold of it.

Alabaster pulled himself up and reached out to seize it. Letting out a furious grunt, Cornelius took hold of his leg. Alabaster wriggled and kicked with all of his might. The stick was within reach, just inches away. But Cornelius's grip was strong, and yanked him backwards. Undeterred, Alabaster stretched out his hand, just brushing the oaken knots with the tips of his fingers.

And then it was snatched away.

To his horror, he looked up to see Kobold towering above him, the staff clenched firmly in his fist.

All was lost.

Cornelius, coughing and spluttering, scrambled to his feet.

'It's true what they say about elves like you,' he spat in Alabaster's direction. 'Disloyal. Disobedient. Disgraceful. Disgusting. But what would one expect of a half-breed Troll?'

A searing pain seemed to explode inside Alabaster's skull as the full force of Cornelius's shoe collided with his face. Suddenly, a dizzying galaxy of black stars clouded his vision and a metallic taste filled his mouth.

'A filthy son-of-an-ogre like you deserves what they get, and make no mistake.'

Another blow landed in the pit of Alabaster's stomach and he convulsed in pain.

He opened his eyes. As the dark shield of spots and spinning lines lifted from his vision, he beheld the blurred forms of Kobold and Cornelius, and the two hundred elves gathered before them gazing in rapture at their master.

Cornelius held out his hand to Kobold. 'Give me the staff.'

Kobold did not move.

'Did you not hear me? I said, give it to me.'

Cornelius reached out to seize it, but Kobold was too quick. The old man gasped to find the butt of it pressed into his stomach.

His eyes bulged in shock and pain.

'Kobold...' he wheezed breathlessly, 'what are you doing?'

With a grunt, Kobold shoved the old man away and he toppled to the floor. Then, brandishing the staff with both hands, he brought it down onto his knee, snapping it clean in two.

Fifty

SANTA'S ARRIVAL

The effect was instantaneous. The elves' eyes rolled back in their heads, their faces turned up, jaws hanging agog. Ghostly green threads of vapour flew out of their mouths and escaped into the night sky.

Too entranced were they to notice an orange mouse suddenly morph into a freckled elf.

'Needles!' Alabaster wheezed, barely able to move. 'It *was* you!'

Needles examined his hands, as if unable to believe his tear-stung eyes.

Coming to, the elves looked at one another, shaking heads in confusion, as though waking from a deep sleep. 'What on earth…? Where are we? What are we doing on the roof?'

Cornelius staggered to his feet and glared at Kobold. 'You...' he snarled. 'You traitor!'

He snatched the halves of the staff from Kobold's hands and tried to push them back together, but it was futile. Whatever magic it had contained was now entirely broken.

Mary seized her chance. 'Cornelius Bandersnatch is a criminal!' she declared through the megaphone. 'We have proof. He has been plotting to steal Christmas to profit himself. We cannot let him succeed!'

In fury, Cornelius charged at her. He seized the lapels of her potato sack and raised her over the heads of the assembled elves, carrying her to the edge of the roof. Twenty floors below, cars the size of matchboxes sped along the main road.

'Help me!' she screamed, her arms slipping through the holes.

Suddenly, a bright light appeared in the distant skies, a trail of sparkling stars in its wake.

'Look there!' one of the elves cried out. Everybody turned to see.

Coasting along the night sky like a shooting star was none other than Santa himself. He was riding on Alabaster's snurfboard!

A great cheer rose from the assembled throng. Cornelius tossed Mary aside onto the asphalt rooftop, where she landed on her back with a thud. Cornelius turned on his heels. He broke into a sprint, each footstep that landed on the air springing him further and further up until he had reached a high platform that rose above the corner of the roof.

'What is he doing?'

At the top of the platform, there seemed to be some sort of control point. Cornelius pressed a pair of binoculars to his eyes, and then fiddled with what looked like a computer joystick. As he did so, Alabaster noticed a movement at the edge of the roof; the rocket that formed part of the building's neon logo was tilting back and forth in time with Cornelius's movements.

It was a missile!

And it was now pointed directly at Santa.

Alabaster could only watch on in horror as the tip of the rocket followed Santa's trajectory.

Suddenly, there was a hiss and a bright flash of light, and the fuse at the base of the rocket ignited, spitting sparks like the end of a sparkler.

'Turn back!' Alabaster cried at the top of his voice.

But Santa could not hear him.

Without levitation powder, he couldn't climb up to the platform and stop Cornelius. What could he do?

In panic, Alabaster looked around for anything he could use.

His eye fell upon the sack, lying just a few feet away.

There was one thing he could do.

He prayed it would work.

He snatched up the sack and staggered behind the airship, where the reindeer were concealed. Alabaster felt his way along the outer reins until he found a pair of antlers. Dasher. He quickly released her from the reins and leapt onto her unsaddled back.

'On Dasher!' he cried, with a gentle kick. 'Dash away, dash away!'

Alabaster clung tightly to the reindeer's antlers as, to a thunder of hooves, they lifted airborne.

Dasher and her passenger continued to climb in circles around the platform. Cornelius was bent over the control panel – he hadn't seen them. Alabaster tore open the sack's neck. At the bottom, the red glowing sands of the Underworld flickered through a circular window. He howled into the void: 'Fluffy! Please help us!'

Clinging tightly to Dasher's antlers with one hand, Alabaster took aim and flung the sack onto the platform. It landed softly and without a sound at Cornelius's heels.

✧ ✧ ✧

The moment Cornelius Bandersnatch had been waiting for his whole life had finally arrived.

'I'm going to get you now!' he snarled with dark excitement. He was grinning like a madman into the binoculars. Behind him, Alabaster saw the sack begin to shake and bulge, and then all at once an enormous creature was rearing out of the sack and breathing onto Cornelius's neck.

Cornelius turned to face the horned beast, dwarfed by its immense size. He gulped as the monster grabbed hold of him by the scruff of his neck. Fluffy let out a mighty roar and tossed him like a ragdoll into the sack. Then the two were gone, bound for the dismal, fiery depths of the Underworld.

The rocket gave a loud whoosh as it launched, sailed right past Santa, and disappeared into space.

Fifty-One

SANTA'S DILEMMA

The elves greeted Santa's arrival onto the rooftop with a chorus of cheers.

'Santa!' Mary ran to him and threw her arms around him. 'You made it just in time. Christmas is saved!'

'I'm afraid not, Mary.' A cloud of sadness passed across Santa's smile. 'It's already five to midnight. There's no way I can make it around the world in time.'

Alabaster's heart sank. Was there really no way?

'What about us?' he said. 'You have two hundred elves at your service, who are more than willing to come and help you.'

Santa let out a mirthless chuckle. 'I'm afraid there's not enough room on my sleigh for two hundred elves, Alabaster.'

'Cornelius has had us building nothing but snurfers for three days,' Mary said. 'We've got more than enough!'

Santa paused. 'That's very unorthodox, are you sure that's not against the rules?'

Bushy stepped forward. 'I'm afraid it is in direct contravention of rule two hundred and forty-six section b of the Elf's Handbook, which clearly states, "Distribution of toys on Christmas Eve is the sole responsibility of S Claus." He looked thoughtful. 'Well… given the circumstances, I'd be willing to overlook it if you would?'

Santa paused. 'Well, perhaps just this once.'

A chorus of elf voices rose in cheer.

'There's just one problem; we don't have any toys.'

Alabaster smiled. 'We've got two hundred elves, we've got two hundred snurfers, we've got levitation powder, we've got the reindeer and we've got you – and we're standing on the roof of one of the biggest toy shops in the world. Everything we need is right here!'

Fifty-Two

THE LOOKING-GLOBE

'There's no need to be nervous,' Mary whispered, leaning in to plant a kiss on Alabaster's cheek. 'You've got this.'

At that moment, a chorus of cheers rang from the crowd hidden on the other side of the red velvet curtain.

Alabaster blushed.

The voice of Bushy Evergreen boomed over the megaphone speakers. 'It gives me great pleasure to welcome an esteemed elf to the stage. An elf whose grit, courage and determination saved Christmas. It would have been very different without him.'

Alabaster dreaded to think what might have been.

Had Cornelius been successful, Christmas would certainly never have been the same again.

From the stage, Bushy's eyes met his own. They were shining now with new warmth.

'Without further ado, ladies and gentlemen,' Bushy said into a microphone, 'it gives me great pleasure to welcome to the stage my new Deputy-Chief Toy Inventor…'

Alabaster drew a sharp breath. At the small of his back, Mary's hand gently ushered him towards the stage.

'…Alabaster Snowball!'

Alabaster climbed the wooden platform. Before him, a crowd of hundreds cheered. It seemed the entire Grotto had turned out for the event.

In the centre of the stage, Bushy extended his hand. The creases at the corners of his ancient eyes crinkled. From the side of the stage, Mary held up both thumbs. There was so much to take in, so many familiar faces… and the seemingly endless roar of cheers. After taking Bushy's hand, the old elf pulled him near.

'Listen to that, Alabaster,' Bushy said in his ear, barely audible above the roar. 'That's all for you.'

Finally, with a calming gesture of the old elf's arm, the cheering gradually abated.

'So, when you came up with this crazy invention,' Bushy said, when all was once again silent, 'who could have known its potential? It saved Christmas Day, no

249

less! I'll be the first to admit, I did not. From escaping the Underworld to delivering the world's presents on Christmas Eve, your invention can be used for anything!

'I misjudged your snurfer, Alabaster, but more importantly, I misjudged you. And for that I am sorry.' Bushy paused, frow burrowed. 'Of course, this item is entirely unsuitable for human hands.'

Alabaster nodded in agreement.

'Nonetheless. Santa and I have discussed it, and we would be honoured to make the Snurfer the Grotto's official mode of transport. With your permission, of course.'

Alabaster did not know what to say. His invention! Bushy knew it was worth something. And, moreover, he was asking his permission. Words did not come easily.

'I – I – I...' he spluttered.

'Is that a yes?'

'Bushy, I would love that!' Alabaster said. Unable to quite control himself, he threw his arms around Bushy and gave him a great big hug.

Bushy laughed awkwardly, and hugged him back. Then he straightened his spectacles and turned his attention once again to the microphone.

'I can confirm that the answer is yes, ladies and gentlemen.'

Once again, the crowd erupted. Even Needles was

smiling up at him. Alabaster bowed his head to the audience with a smile and turned to leave the stage.

'No, no, Alabaster – that's not all. I know there is someone else who would like to speak to you. Look.'

Bushy directed Alabaster's eyes to the sky, and every elf in the crowd followed his gaze.

Floating through the clear winter skies, in the direction of the stage, was none other than Santa himself, a trail of sparkles following the snurfer he rode upon.

He swooped neatly onto the boards to join Bushy and Alabaster, looking resplendent in his best crimson Christmas outfit.

'In recognition of your services to the Grotto,' Santa said, as he retrieved a small box from his jacket's inside pocket, 'it gives me great pleasure to reward your efforts with this.'

He prised open the box to reveal a shiny star pin made of solid gold. On it were written the words *Official Medal of Courage.*

To the sound of cheers, Santa removed the medal from its box and pinned it to Alabaster's lapel.

He gestured to a microphone, encouraging Alabaster to speak. The assembly began to chant: 'Speech, speech, speech...' until Alabaster felt he had no choice but to approach the podium.

'I am so grateful Santa. And Bushy. I really am... but I'm afraid I can't accept this award.'

A hush fell over the crowd.

Alabaster felt a weight in his tummy.

'First of all, I didn't save Christmas single-handedly. It took all of us – every single one – to make sure all the presents were delivered on time. But more than that, I have to be honest. If it weren't for me, Cornelius would never have found the location of the Grotto in the first place.'

With a look of sorrow, Alabaster unfastened the medal from his lapel and extended it towards its giver it in his clasped hand.

'And my name would never have appeared on the Naughty List.'

The crowd waited on baited breath.

Santa, smiling, produced a familiar maroon box from within his crimson coat. 'You mean this, Alabaster?'

With a flick of his wrist, the scroll's gilded parchment unravelled to the floor and bounced along the stage.

Santa smiled. 'Take a look.'

Alabaster followed the scroll until he reached the 'S's.

He gawped.

Beneath the Snodgrasses, Snoebergers, Snoswells and Snotts, his name was nowhere to be seen.

'But… how?'

'If there is a lesson to be learned in all of this,' Santa said, placing a hand on Alabaster's shoulder. 'It is this:

all mistakes are forgivable if one has the courage to admit them… and strive to make them right.'

'I –'

'Which you did. You thought only of others and how to bring them the greatest happiness… that, truly, is what Christmas is all about.'

He took the pin from Alabaster and pinned it once again to his lapel with a smile.

'Please accept the honour. You deserve it.'

※ ※ ※

'Can I open my eyes now?'

'Not yet. Hold still.'

Mary barely breathed as Alabaster whisked off a dustcloth with a swoosh.

'Ok,' he said finally. 'Now.'

Mary lifted her blindfold and let out a gasp.

'What *is* that?'

In Alabaster's living room, on a plinth of about four feet in height, sat a very large dome of white crystal.

'Just something I've been working on. I call it the Looking Globe.'

Mary leaned in for closer examination. Inside the clear glass bubble lay a carpet of snowflakes.

'How does it work?' Mary asked.

'You think of the thing you want to see most of all

in the world...' Alabaster closed his eyes. 'Then you do this.' He placed his hand on the crystalline surface. 'Show me Santa!'

In the bell of the Looking Globe, the particles began to dance and whirl, until they became a tornado of flurrying white spots. The flakes collected into the centre before settling into an astonishingly lifelike image of Santa. He was smiling, and even the flurrying flecks were somehow able to capture his trademark twinkle.

'Hey Santa!' Mary said, giving the figure a wave. 'It looks so real!'

'That's him. And look, there's Dasher too.'

Mary turned her eyes to Alabaster. 'And what about the krampus?'

Alabaster smiled and held his hand over the glass orb. 'Show me Fluffy.'

Once again, the snowflakes flurried and flew before settling into the shape of a very contented krampus, frolicking in the Underworld's ash and dust like an excitable dog.

'I bet you must really miss him, huh?'

Alabaster nodded. 'The good thing is I can still see him every day. That's the best thing about the Looking Globe; it allows me to keep an eye on Fluffy, but without breaking the Elf Handbook's guidelines. I'm not keeping him at the Grotto, so...'

'Alabaster, are you sure that's allowed?'

'It's never shown up on the Naughty List, so I figure it's ok.' He offered a shrug. 'But let's not broadcast it, if that's all right with you?'

'I won't tell Bushy, if that's what you mean.'

Alabaster smiled.

'Speaking of which, I'd better be getting off home.' She gave Alabaster the warmest of hugs.

'Happy new year, Mary.'

When she was gone, Alabaster returned to the Looking Globe. He held out his hand. In a low voice, he said, 'Show me Father.'

When the flakes had settled, they revealed a solitary figure hunched against the cold, carrying a large haversack. It appeared as though he were climbing a mountain, with a large stick in either hand. Wherever he was, it was nowhere Alabaster recognised in Lapland, and it was certainly no longer London. Other figures came into the scene, greeting Kobold. Wild Elves. Kobold had returned to the wilds of Oslo.

Alabaster thought about him occasionally. The strange ties that prevented the old Wild Elf causing him harm. And the fact that it was Kobold himself that had ended up releasing them from Nixie's spell. Nixie, who was no longer at his side.

She, it transpired, remained a cockroach.

Quite why she did not return to elf-form with the

breaking of the staff, Alabaster could not say. But he resisted the urge to ever look again.

He knew he had Santa. He had Mary, and even Bushy.

And, thanks to the portal sack, he still had Fluffy.

He had a family of his own that loved him, and that was all that mattered.

Epilogue

NEXT CHRISTMAS

In the depths of the Underworld, Cornelius seethed.

It had been a year. And a year in the Underworld was a very long time. A veritable eternity, in fact, with little to do except sit and grumble to himself and watch his own hair turn grey.

Occasionally, the elf that had got him into this mess would come and visit. Not to visit him, of course, but the revolting creature.

What was it Kobold had called it? The krampus? The Wild Elf called it 'Fluffy'.

From the distance of his small rocky island, marooned within a moat of molten lava, Cornelius watched the krampus and Alabaster interact.

Over countless nights that stretched into infinity, he had witnessed Alabaster trying to teach the krampus to read. Several books had not survived his early attempts, but eventually the creature appeared to learn that books were for reading and not eating.

He had watched Alabaster bring food for the creature. Great big slabs of cooked meat, but not a bite for Cornelius. True, he did not seem to need to eat or drink down here, but it would have relieved the boredom. He had to make do with the occasional dead carcass of a bat that fell from the cavernous roof, where nests of them hung above. The one benefit of living in the Underworld was that there was no end to sources of heat for cooking the bat-meat. And bat blood wasn't so bad once you got accustomed to the strange tang.

Sometimes he pitied himself that this was what he had been reduced to – a miserable scavenger. These days, he bathed himself in anger and wallowed in fantasies of revenge and retribution.

On other days, he applauded himself for being able to endure anything. Such days, he told himself he was a *survivor*.

One day, Alabaster brought the Krampus a newspaper. The blistering headline attacking Santa, clearly the handiwork of one Wilhelmina Turnpike, brought a touch of actual joy to Cornelius's day.

It was good to know that she was keeping up the good work in his absence.

Not long after that the krampus disappeared and came back with a surprise.

Suddenly, Cornelius was no longer alone. A person – a woman – was crumpled in the volcanic sand beside him.

When she had scuttled to her feet, Cornelius recognised her instantly.

Wilhelmina Turnpike.

'Cornelius?' she said, adjusting her glasses in disbelief. 'Is that really you?'

But Cornelius was too fixated on an item of Wilhelmina's attire to respond.

'That necklace,' he stammered. 'Where did you get it?'

Wilhelmina clasped the jewel to her chest, seemingly alarmed by the fire in Cornelius's eyes. 'What's it to you?'

'Tell me, damn it!' Cornelius wheezed.

With a kiss of the teeth, Wilhelmina relented. 'After your servant Nixie disappeared with her husband, it seemed she had no further need of it. Would have been a shame to let such a beautiful thing go to waste. Brings out the colour in my eyes, don't you think?'

Cornelius, however, cast his gaze towards the nest of bats that encircled the eye to the Grotto.

'If this is what I think it is, my dear,' he grinned dangerously, 'then we have ourselves an opportunity.'

His eyes returned to the mouth at the roof of the cave.

'And a way out...'

. . . But that's a story for another Christmas.

Acknowledgements

With huge thanks to Anna Bowles & Amber Hatch for their consummate editorial guidance and professional insight – it has been an education and a privilege.

Thanks also to my beta readers for making the time and effort to not just read the book's early drafts, but offer detailed comments and feedback. This book is far better thanks to you. Special thanks to Zella Compton, Gemma and Reuben Walker, Caitlyn Burt, Emily Davis, Fiona Coffey, Liza Keast, Karen Newby, Amanda Bird, Fabio Barros and Nichola Rivers.

With immense thanks to Pedro Fama for his gorgeous cover illustration and design, which truly exceeded all expectations and really help bring the characters to life.

Thanks also to Mike Bugg and the staff at Universal Enterprises Inc for granting kind permission for the use of *character names – I hope I've done Alabaster and Mary proud.*

And finally, to all the children I have had the pleasure of teaching, and for all they've had to teach me in return. With special thanks to Ariane and Miguel of St Cyprian's Primary Academy for being the book's first middle-grade audience.